Undercurrents

WILLO DAVIS ROBERTS

ALADDIN PAPERBACKS

New York London Toronto Sydney Singapore

First Aladdin Paperbacks edition August 2003
Text copyright © 2002 by Willo Davis Roberts

ALADDIN PAPERBACKS
An imprint of Simon & Schuster
Children's Publishing Division
1230 Avenue of the Americas
New York, NY 10020

Also available in an Atheneum Books for Young Readers hardcover edition.
Designed by Michael Nelson
The text of this book was set in Lomba.

Printed in the United States of America
6 8 10 9 7

The Library of Congress has cataloged the hardcover edition as follows:
Roberts, Willo Davis.
Undercurrents / Willo Davis Roberts.
p. cm.
Summary: Fourteen-year-old Nikki has trouble accepting
her new stepmother Crystal, and the problem grows worse when they visit
the northern California house where Crystal lived as a child and experienced
some horrible event that she is trying to keep secret.
ISBN 0-689-81671-5 (hc.)
[1. Stepmothers—Fiction. 2. California—Fiction.
3. Mystery and detective stories.] I. Title.
PZ7.R54465   Un 2002
[Fic]—dc21 2001022989
ISBN 0-689-85994-5 (Aladdin pbk.)

To my grandaughter Jessie

1

It was supposed to be the summer we went to Europe. My parents had been saving and planning for it for at least two years, and it would be our last grand adventure before my sister, Bonnie, went off to college, while we were all still together as a family.

Even after she got so sick, Mama continued to pore over the travel brochures and the maps, plotting out our journey. I'd sit beside her on the bed, and we'd discuss the merits of hotels and museums we must see, and the most worthwhile churches to include in our itinerary.

"Not just the cathedrals, the big, fancy ones," Mama told me earnestly, "but the little churches in the small towns or out in the country. The kind of churches we'd go to on a regular basis if we lived near them."

We talked about clothes. We'd be flying over, so we couldn't plan to take a lot of stuff. We'd need comfortable shoes, and lightweight sweaters or jackets, and walking shorts and pants and shirts and underwear that could be washed out and could dry overnight. And at least one somewhat dressy outfit for each of us, for occasions when casual wear wouldn't be appropriate, like special dinners or religious observances.

We'd spent one afternoon like this, and at the dinner table—this was after Mom had stopped joining us, saying that it tired her out too much, and she'd rather have her meals in bed—I was talking about a place Mom especially wanted to see. I was enthusiastic about it too, until I intercepted the glance Bonnie sent at Dad.

I stopped in mid-sentence. "What?" I demanded.

Bonnie swallowed, then licked her lips. "Nikki—do you really not know?"

"Know what?" I asked.

"That it isn't going to happen. We're not going to go."

Bewildered, I looked at Dad. "But you promised! And we've planned for so long—"

Dad didn't say anything, just looked at me. With such pain in his eyes, such compassion. And a total inability to put into words what Bonnie was telling me.

"She's never going to be well enough to go, Nick," Bonnie said softly.

Beside me, ten-year-old Sam slurped at his milk, and for once nobody corrected him. He was thinking about his Little League game later on, and he didn't even hear what we were talking about.

And for the first time, I realized the truth. My mother was dying.

At that moment, it was the worst possible thing I could think of.

Until Dad brought home a new wife only eight months after Mama died. Until he shipped us off to Trinidad, California, for the summer, and I learned new depths of bewilderment and loneliness and fear.

Before finishing growing up from what I thought of as a fairly mature fourteen-year-old into an adult world of suspicion and secrets and numbing horror robbed me of what was supposed to have been the most wonderful summer of my life.

Somehow we got through losing Mama.

It was in the winter, and it rained every day those last few weeks, including the day of the funeral. I didn't go with Dad to make the arrangements at the funeral home; Bonnie did that. She came home with red eyes and told me not to bother Dad when he went into his room—the one where Mama had died—and she made toasted cheese sandwiches and tomato soup for supper later.

Everybody tried to be brave. Grandma Simons came to Seattle from Boise, and Grandpa and Grandma Booker from Sacramento, and for a couple of days the house was full of people. Aunts and uncles and cousins. People from the church brought food to feed them all, and nobody had to worry about cooking anything.

Not that we'd done all that much cooking for quite a while, before. Mama got so she could hardly eat even the things she'd always liked, and the rest of us lost our appetites, too, except for Sam. I guess at ten nothing shuts down your appetite.

He did talk to me a little, after Grandma Simons came that last week.

"How come the doctors can't make her better?" he asked, leaning his head into my chest.

"I don't know," I said honestly. "They tried, but it didn't work."

And then, the morning Mama actually died, and the van carrying her body had driven away and the hospice lady began gathering up her things to leave for the last time, Sam came to me again. "Grandma says," he told me, "that Mama's gone on to a better place."

"Yeah, I guess," I agreed.

"Where she won't hurt anymore."

"That ends when someone dies," I told him, my throat aching. How did people stand it, losing their loved ones this way? Why didn't we just all die at once and get it over with, and not leave any of this agony?

"So Mama's better off, like Grandma says. Right?" Sam asked.

"Right," I told him. But what about the rest of us? We certainly weren't better off. Even during the months when she was so sick, we were better off with her. And even though Mama had been only one person, out of a family of five, it now seemed as if there was nothing left of the Simons family.

We got through the funeral, with the rain dripping onto the casket covered with yellow roses, and squishing back to the limousine and soaking my shoes so that when I got home and took them off, I threw them in the trash, unwilling to ever wear them again.

Once more the church ladies came to our rescue with casseroles and homemade rolls and salads and cakes and pies. More than we could ever eat, even with all the grandparents and aunts and uncles and cousins there. Grandma Booker put a lot of stuff in the freezer for later.

My Sunday school teacher, Mrs. Setzer, brought something wrapped in foil and stopped to give me a wordless hug after she'd deposited it in the kitchen. I was glad for her touch, but I really only remembered it later. At the time I was simply too numb to register much.

And eventually everybody went away, and Dad went back to work reading manuscripts he had brought home from the publishing company where he was an editorial director. We kids went back to school. Bonnie applied to go to Western Washington University in Bellingham. She had decided to live on campus, even though she could have commuted if she'd really wanted to. Dad offered to get her a car so she could, but she turned him down. "I'd rather live in the dorm with Beth and Jessie and the rest of them," she said, and he didn't insist.

"Why, Bonnie?" I begged her when we sat cross-legged on our beds while she made out a list of things she would want to take. "We need you here!"

"I have to get away, Nick," my sister said. "Maybe it'll help, having a complete change of scene, a total lifestyle change. You'll manage. You're fourteen. I wasn't an awful lot older than that when Mom got sick, remember."

But I wasn't Bonnie. I was the second child, the one who was not "the pretty one," or "the smartest one." I couldn't even cook toasted sandwiches without scorching them. I forgot to defrost meat in time to get it cooked for supper. I left a red sock in with the white clothes and Dad was ticked when his underwear came out pink. I didn't know what to do when Sam scraped up his elbow and needed a few stitches. I couldn't drive and had to call a taxi to take us to the walk-in clinic, and then they wouldn't do anything until Dad came and signed the papers. It seemed like I was just useless.

"It's not going to work, Bonnie," I said. "You were only gone a week this time, checking out the college. What'll I do when you're gone permanently?"

Bonnie hugged me and smiled. "You'll manage, Nick. The same as I did. I didn't know everything at fourteen either. Remember the time I microwaved the roast and it came out like such a rock that even Buster wouldn't eat it?"

Buster was our black Lab, and he was so old, his teeth weren't good enough to chew rocks. We'd thrown the roast over the fence into the Benitos' yard, and their rottweiler made short work of it. We never told Dad; we just opened a big can of chili for supper and he never knew the difference. Mom had told us the secret of pepping up a second-rate meal, like canned chili. *Make corn bread to go with it,* she'd said, *or Bisquick biscuits. Dad'll be so pleased with those, he won't even know what else he's eating.*

Bonnie had learned to pacify Dad in all kinds of

situations. Of course after Mom got sick I don't think he gave too much thought to what he was eating. He never complained, even when we had tuna casserole—not his favorite—three days running.

Bonnie got an after-school job for her last year of high school, to save up to help pay for college. "It'll be good practice for you, Nikki," she told me. "Before I move out of the house entirely."

I despaired of ever learning to cope. I wasn't any good at housework. I didn't seem to notice dust unless somebody wrote their name in it. I'd forget to run laundry until somebody announced they were out of socks or underwear or towels. Everything I cooked came out burned unless I was just reheating it in the microwave. I couldn't remember to get what we needed from the grocery store. If we didn't have all the ingredients for a recipe, I had no idea what to substitute. A couple of times I dumped the results into the garbage before anybody else had a chance to taste it. I figured if Buster stuck up his nose at it, it wasn't worth eating.

During the time Mama was sick, my friends sort of fell by the wayside. So much of the time I couldn't get away to do the things I'd always done with other kids, and gradually they stopped asking me. After she was gone, I didn't have the heart for most things, and my closest friends were already best buds with other people.

And then Dad came home one night and sat us down at the table, not even waiting until we'd eaten dinner. All three of us. "I have something to tell you, kids," he said, and he was smiling a little.

We waited, expectant. Well, sort of, on my part. I didn't think he'd won the lottery or we'd inherited a million dollars or anything. We didn't have any rich relatives. And even money couldn't have made up for losing Mom.

Dad's smile widened as he looked around at us. "I'm getting married next month," he said, as if it were the most wonderful thing in the world.

If I'd had any idea what was coming, I'd have tried not to look as if a horse had just kicked me in the stomach.

Bonnie's mouth had dropped open, though she quickly closed it. Sam kicked his heels against his chair and said, "Who to?"

"Her name's Crystal," Dad said. His gaze swung to me. "You'll like her, kids. She's a wonderful lady."

I could hardly get enough breath to speak. "But . . . it's not even a year since Mom died! Eight months, actually."

"I know that, honey. But I've met this wonderful girl. She's an artist, the illustrator for a book we're doing. She came into the office to have a consultation with the art director, and we met. She's . . . she won me over, immediately."

"When did you meet her?" Bonnie asked. I thought she sounded sort of wooden. Maybe the horse had kicked her in the stomach too; she was just better than I was at covering it up.

"Before Mama died?" I said before I could stop myself.

Something flickered in Dad's eyes. Pain again? "No. Not before Mom died. About three months ago."

"And you're getting married already?" I couldn't help it, my voice squeaked with indignation.

Dad reached for my hand and covered it with his own. "Nikki, please try to understand. I fell in love with her. We want to be together."

I felt my heart growing harder, so that it made my chest ache. "If you loved Mama, how could you already be in love with someone else?"

His hand was big and warm as he squeezed mine. "I did love Mom, you know I did. When I realized she was dying, I thought I might die myself, it hurt so much. And from that point on, I had to begin letting go of her. Can you understand that? My grief started a long time before she actually passed away. My life had revolved around her, and it continued to while we were taking care of her, but it wasn't the same. She became another of my children, not my wife any longer. I loved her until her last breath, and I'll always love her in my heart.

But I need a wife, honey. Someone to live with, and touch, and do things with."

"You've got us, Dad," Sam pointed out.

"And I thank God for you, all three of you. But having children is not the same as having a wife. I need a wife, kids."

"For sex," I said brutally, and saw my sister's quick intake of air.

His face got a little red, then, but he didn't let go of my hand, and his expression showed no shame. "That, too, of course, but that's only a part of why a man needs a wife. You kids will grow up and leave home. Bonnie's already planning to leave right after graduation. It won't be long before you and Sam are out of school, too. Your mother and I planned to grow old together, to keep each other company, to enjoy the same things for the rest of our lives. And now that isn't going to happen. But I've met Crystal. And I think it can happen with her, so I've asked her to marry me."

The cold, hard thing in my chest was killing me. It couldn't be true, I thought. He couldn't really be saying these things. He couldn't have forgotten Mama so soon.

"I'll bring her out to meet you next weekend," Dad was saying now, as I sat there resenting his every word. "I know you're going to love each other."

I knew we weren't. I knew I was going to hate her.

I could see Bonnie and Sam digesting all of this, trying to accept what Dad was saying.

I didn't accept it. Nothing could have been worse than this, nothing, to ruin all our lives.

It just goes to show how you can underestimate a situation. Naturally, it got even worse.

2

"How can he be in love with her?" I practically spat the words at my sister. "She isn't even pretty!"

Bonnie nibbled on a fingernail. "Pretty isn't everything, Nick. She's probably very nice, once you get to know her. Unfortunately, we didn't make much progress in that direction today. I suspect she feels like she met the family from hell."

"Mostly due to me, you mean." I didn't care. I was even more angry now than I'd been when Dad told us about her. "What was I supposed to do? Kiss up to her? Act like I was happy she was planning to marry Dad, when Mom is hardly cold?"

Bonnie sighed. "That's not true, Nikki. Mom's dead

and buried, and she's never coming back. We're not going to forget her, but she isn't going to be a part of our everyday lives anymore. There's something to what Dad says. He needs a wife, and we're not the ones who have to be in love with her, if *he* is."

"We're the ones who'll have to live with her."

"It won't be forever. I mean, you'll be out of school and gone in just a few years."

"That's easy for you to say, when you're leaving practically the minute you graduate. I'll have at least four more years!"

"Nikki, how long was Mom sick?"

I stared at her. "More than a year. What's that got to do with it?"

"We got through it. All of us. It was horrible, especially after we knew she was never going to get better. But we *survived* it. And it's now past and done with. The same will be true of whatever else that comes up that needs to be dealt with. Including Dad marrying Crystal. Just make up your mind to make the best of it. I know it doesn't seem fair that I'm going to be able to get away from it and you can't. But I don't know what else to tell you except to stick it out."

My eyes filled, blurring my vision. "I don't know if I can, Bonnie. I can't believe he's going to marry somebody practically the same age as his own kids! She's only fourteen years older than I am! How are you going to feel, introducing her as your *mother* when she looks like your *sister?*"

Bonnie's only indication of tension was that she kept chewing on a fingernail. "I won't introduce her as my mother. I'll just say her name: Crystal. If they don't get it, I'll add, *My father's wife.* That ought to do it."

"I can't believe you're taking it so calmly. Doesn't it make you *hurt,* in here?" I put my fingers against my chest and struggled with tears that refused to be held back.

"Yes," Bonnie admitted. "But remember what Mom said? Even if it hurts terribly, if there's nothing you can do to change things, you just accept it and get on with it, no matter how difficult it is."

"She meant dying," I choked. "This feels almost as bad as dying."

"But there was no way to stop it, so she did it. And we suffered along with her and felt like dying, too, but we couldn't, so here we are. Left over, after she's gone. And now we have to help Dad, because he's left behind too, and he's been hurting as much as we have. And if it makes him feel better to marry Crystal, then we just have to accept it."

Misery welled up inside of me until I couldn't control

the sobs that rose to the surface. I put my face in my hands and cried.

She slid off her bed and onto mine and put her arms around me, hugging me tight. After awhile we pulled apart, and she reached for the tissue box. I took a handful and blew my nose.

"She's probably not so bad," Bonnie said, "when you get used to her."

But I didn't know if I ever could.

Dad didn't do a very good job of planning our first meeting with our stepmother-to-be. To begin with, he didn't spring it on us until we'd all made other plans for that Saturday.

Bonnie was going shopping for clothes to wear on a trip to Washington, D.C., with three other girls. She protested, but Dad spoke with unusual firmness.

"I've already arranged it with Crystal, and I need all of you to be there," he said.

Indecision played across her face. "That means I'll have to disappoint everybody else when I don't show up. Either they'll have to rearrange their plans at the last minute, or go without me, and then I'd have to go alone later."

"This is important to me," Dad said, and we both knew that meant he wasn't going to give her any way out of it, no matter how unfair it seemed to her.

"I've got ball practice," Sam objected when he was informed.

"You can afford to miss practice for once," said our father, who didn't usually let anyone weasel out of any commitment. "It'll be a good opportunity for that new kid to show what he can do at first base."

"But what if he's better than I am and they kick me off that position?" Sam demanded.

"Then," Dad said cold-bloodedly, "you'll just have to get better enough to win it back."

And then there was me. I knew I didn't have a chance, but I had to try. "I was planning to spend Saturday at the library getting out that last report for History. It'll count a lot toward my final grade," I said.

"Nikki, give me a break. You can go to the library anytime you want, only just not on Saturday. I promised Crystal a picnic, and we're going to have one. Period."

Short of suicide, there didn't seem to be any way out of it. We, Dad informed us, would be packing the lunch.

He gave us the menu. Fried chicken, baked beans, potato salad, pickles, and corn bread. With chocolate cake and Jell-O with bananas and marshmallows for dessert.

Bonnie pointed out that corn bread was best right from the oven, and that it was kind of crumbly to carry along on a picnic.

"I like it fine after it's cold," Dad said flatly. "If a lot of crumbs fall on the ground, the ants will find them and have their own picnic."

So we followed his orders. We scorched the chicken a little bit, but Dad made sure Crystal didn't get one of those pieces. Sam made the lemonade, and he got too much water in it and not enough sugar, but everybody drank it without comment.

Dad went to get Crystal in Seattle while we were finishing up. We were all waiting on the front porch when they drove up in the van and parked. Dad got out and came around the front of the car to open the door for her, just the way he used to do with Mama before she got too sick to go anywhere.

My stomach tightened in a knot. How could he stand to do this? Didn't it remind him, too, of what we'd had?

It didn't seem to be bothering him. He was wearing shorts and a knit shirt, and for a guy who was forty-six years old, he looked pretty great. Mom used to tease him that she'd married him for his sexy legs. Everything I remembered was like an ice pick stuck in my heart.

Crystal got out of the car. The first thing I noticed was that she was skinny. She was wearing shorts, too, and a matching blue-and-white-striped shirt and white sandals. If I'd been her, I'd have worn long pants just to keep people from seeing how untanned and how thin I was.

Dad touched her elbow and guided her toward us, coming to a stop at the foot of the porch steps. "Hi, kids. This is Crystal." He was beaming as if he'd just brought us a Christmas present.

We all said "hi" back. Not even Bonnie could put a lot of enthusiasm into it.

She wasn't pretty. She wasn't homely, either, just kind of ordinary. Mom had been beautiful before she got sick.

Crystal had one striking feature, however. Her hair was a sort of silvery gilt blond, with just a hint of a wave at each temple, and otherwise quite straight. It was cut very short, almost like mine.

Mine, however, was plain old brown, and even Mom had never been able to figure out how to do anything to make it behave, except cut most of it off.

For a moment, I almost envied Crystal's pale hair.

She was staring up at us, not quite smiling.

"Hi, everybody. I hope we didn't keep you waiting."

Her voice was very soft and somewhat high-pitched, the kind of voice I'd always thought sounded affected. Bonnie said later it was probably more pronounced than usual because she was nervous. I didn't see what she had to be nervous about—not as much as *we* had—but maybe Bonnie was right.

"We have to go with you, anyway, so it doesn't matter," Sam said. "Haven't you got any kids?"

She moistened her lips. "No. I've never been married or had a family."

"Bummer," Sam noted, and Dad said, "Well, now she'll have all three of you. Lunch all packed?"

Bonnie nudged the picnic basket forward. "All ready. Sam, I think you'd better hit the bathroom before we go."

He was used to this directive, and took off at once. Crystal moistened her lips again. She was wearing very pale lipstick. "We're going to a park, right? Maybe I should use your rest room before we leave, too."

"Sure," Dad said heartily. "Nikki can show you where it is."

She followed close behind me. I could smell her perfume, something light and very different from what Mom had liked. We had to wait for Sam to leave the bathroom, and then I hesitated, wondering if I should wait for her.

What the heck, I decided. She was an adult. She could surely find her way back to the front door by herself.

Dad was stowing the basket and the gallon thermos in the back of the van. Bonnie turned when I came out onto the porch. Neither of us said anything for a few minutes. Then I observed, "She's sure taking a long time. She's probably checking out the medicine chest and making sure the sink is clean."

"So what?" Bonnie asked. "She's going to live here pretty soon, so it'll be her house, too. And I cleaned the sink myself, so I know it'll pass inspection."

Crystal came out then, and we all went to the car. She sat in the front with Dad, so they could talk. Sam sat in the backseat, as usual, which wasn't necessarily a good idea, since he got the lid off the pickle jar and spilled juice onto his shorts when nobody was looking.

Bonnie and I sat in the middle seat, where we could hear most of what Dad and Crystal were saying but weren't expected to join in the conversation. It was just as well, because a lot of it was sickening.

"Look, sweetheart, you can see the mountains from here," Dad said. How could she have lived in Seattle and never noticed that we were surrounded by mountains? "That's Mount Pilchuck over there. On the way home, we'll be able to catch a glimpse of Mount Baker to the north. Did you know it's actually a volcano?"

"I hope it never erupts," Crystal said. Well, *duh*, I thought.

He called her *sweetheart* four times in a fifteen-minute drive. He could have been driving nails into me. I muttered something to Bonnie about it, under my breath, and she gave me a direct look. "He always called Mom *honey*. Would it make you feel better or worse if he called her *that?*"

The park on Blackman Lake wasn't a very good choice for this picnic. There was nothing in particular to do except sit and look at one another, if we weren't content with admiring the ducks on the water.

"I think," Bonnie said as we waited for Dad and Crystal to decide whether to take our stuff to a table out in the sun or to one of the shaded ones in the pavilion, "that's the point. He wants us to get acquainted with her. And her to learn about us."

They decided to go undercover. Crystal had fair skin, and she hadn't been out in the sun much so far this year. We'd brought a tablecloth and spread it out on a table next to a family of twelve, or maybe it was a reunion or something. They were very noisy.

"I wish you'd have let me bring something," Crystal said as we unloaded the basket.

"Didn't need to," Dad assured her. "My girls are both good cooks."

What a lie *that* was. Bonnie wasn't too bad, but I certainly didn't qualify. Why try to fool her? She'd soon realize that I wasn't a particularly good any-thing, except a bookworm. I wondered if she was a reader or one of those people who think reading's a waste of time.

I addressed her directly for the first time. "Do you like books?"

Dad laughed. "What a question! Crystal illustrates books for some of my authors."

He always spoke of them as *his* authors. I wondered how the authors themselves felt about that. The ones we'd met, though, seemed to be pleased to have him as their editor, so maybe that was okay.

"I meant to *read*," I managed.

"Oh, I enjoy reading. When I can find time," Crystal said.

Real readers *made* time for an essential activity, but with Dad standing right there I didn't think it was a good time to say so. I lifted the Jell-O salad bowl out of the basket, and somehow it twisted in my hands and the lid came off, and part of it spilled right down Crystal's front.

I grabbed desperately for the lid and got the bowl upright, staring in horror at bright red clingy bits all over the blue-and-white-striped shirt. "I'm sorry! I'm sorry, the lid isn't supposed to come off, but it did! And it's kind of runny. I guess we should have made it last night instead of this morning, so it would have been more solid—" I ran out of breath, and I could see the fury rising in Dad's face. I grabbed a handful of the paper towels we'd brought for napkins and started to reach out to clean off the mess, then handed them to her instead. Somehow swabbing the bosom of a lady I'd just met seemed a bit too personal.

"I'm sorry!" I gasped one more time, not knowing what else to do. A banana slice slid off her shirt and dropped onto the concrete slab beneath the table, and I dove for it. My elbow caught on the corner of the corn bread pan, and over it went too. It landed upside down beside the banana slice.

"Don't pick it up!" Bonnie said quickly. "There's plastic wrap over it, so if we're careful, we can salvage it without it getting dirty."

It wasn't dirty, but it sure bore out our expectations about being crumbly. Except that being in small pieces made it hard to butter, it tasted all right.

Dad was looking with dismay at Crystal's shirt. "It never occurred to me I ought to tell you to bring an extra shirt," he said. "I didn't expect my kids to attack you."

I gave a moan of protest, and Sam announced loudly that *he* hadn't had anything to do with it.

"It was an accident, Jeff," Crystal said. "Is there running water in that rest room?"

We assured her there was, and she went off to remove her shirt and try to rinse it out. Of course she didn't have anything to change into, so she had to come back wearing it wet and looking something like the underwear did after it got washed with the red sock, but it was better than actual globs of gelatin sticking to her.

It had been an uncomfortable period, while she was gone, though Dad hadn't accused me of dumping the Jell-O deliberately. Luckily—or perhaps unluckily—I had a reputation for being a klutz. Mom had assured me I'd grow out of it, but so far I wasn't showing any sign of such a thing.

"These beans are delicious," Crystal said when we finally got to eat. She looked from me to Bonnie, seeking the maker.

"It was Mom's recipe," Bonnie and I said at the same time, and then I glanced at Dad to see if that, too, was a no-no.

Apparently not. He shoveled in a forkful himself. "Pam was a wonderful cook," he told Crystal, so I figured out it wasn't going to be forbidden to speak about Mom in her presence. "Of course, that last year or so she wasn't able to do much, but she passed the recipes along to the girls."

"Are you a good cook?" Sam asked her, leaning forward so that his shirt dragged in the potato salad.

A faint pink touched Crystal's cheeks. "Not very, I guess. I only have a few favorite recipes that I do well. I guess I'll have to learn."

"Didn't your mom give you her recipes?" Sam persisted.

I happened to be watching Crystal at that moment, and I guess I was the only one who saw the peculiar expression there for a matter of seconds.

Was I the only one who detected—or thought I did—the faint tremor in her voice when she replied?

"I never really knew my real mother. She . . . died when I was only seven."

"Wow! Just like us," Sam said. "Did your dad take care of you by himself, then?"

I had forgotten to eat, observing her. Was she simply nervous, the way Bonnie said? Was this really an ordeal for her, as if we were testing her, interrogating her with hostile intent?

I felt a moment of repentance, because maybe it *did* sound that way, though I honestly didn't believe any of us meant to be hostile. We were still grieving for Mama, we hadn't yet accepted Dad's decision to get married again, and of course we didn't know anything about Crystal. Weren't we supposed to be getting acquainted with her? And how else could we do that except by asking questions?

Crystal definitely hesitated before she responded to Sam, though I didn't see why. Surely she could remember who had raised her.

"No. My father died too."

Sam's eyes flew wide open. "At the same time as your mother? Holy cow! Were they in an accident?"

Everybody was looking at her by this time. Was her face chalky, or was it just that it never had much color?

She ran her tongue over her lips and reached for a spoonful of corn bread crumbs to put on her paper plate. "Yes," she said finally. "An accident."

"How horrible!" Bonnie breathed, and Dad covered Crystal's hand where it rested in her lap.

"Was it a car accident?" Sam demanded, and Dad gave him a quelling glance.

"That's enough, Sam. That's a hard thing to talk about, I'm sure. We don't need to know all the details, do we?"

"Did you have to go into a foster home, then?" Sam said, irrepressible.

Dad didn't object to that one. After all, getting us together to learn about one another had been *his* idea.

"It was an aunt who took you in, wasn't it, sweetheart?"

"Yes." Crystal gave up trying to butter crumbs and instead put a bit of butter on her spoon and then scooped up a mouthful. "I was with her for only about six months, though, and then I was put up for adoption. So I grew up with an adopted family."

"Did it feel strange, to be adopted?" Sam wanted to know.

"No. It felt nice," Crystal said, though she wasn't smiling about it. "They were very good to me. They even took me to a counselor and helped me . . . get over becoming an orphan."

I wasn't sure she'd meant to add that last part, about a counselor. There was an uncertainty on her face. Of course I could understand why she might have needed one, after losing both parents at once. Thinking of losing Dad, too, was enough to fill me with deep horror.

"Why didn't your aunt keep you? Instead of having you adopted?" Sam asked, almost forgetting to eat.

"She was an older woman. Unmarried. She thought I'd be better off with a family."

"Were there other kids in the family, then?" Nothing but a strip of tape over his mouth was going to shut him up, apparently.

"No. They couldn't have children of their own, so they took me."

Dad still had his hand over hers. "I'll bet you were a charming little girl."

"I was a very lost little girl, to begin with," Crystal said in that very soft voice.

"Who grew into a charming young woman," Dad said, squeezing her hand before setting her free to continue eating.

She complimented everything, even the slightly scorched chicken, but I noticed she didn't really eat very much. I think it was as much a relief to her as it was to us when Dad decided to pack up the leftovers and head for home.

During the last half hour we were at the park, some boys came and built a ramp at the edge of the water, then raced their bikes out and catapulted into the water on them. Dad didn't object when we went over to watch them. He only commented that if a kid of his put a good bike into the lake that way, he'd expect them to pay for the next one, because he certainly wouldn't do it.

I think he was glad we left him to sit and talk with Crystal by herself. I think she was glad we went away, at least a short distance.

When we were getting back in the car to leave, I pulled my final disaster of the day. I managed to slam a door on her fingers.

They turned blue-black immediately and swelled up like cooking sausages.

She let out a surprised yelp, and Dad jerked the door open and off her hand, and I stood by once more humiliated, embarrassed, and apologetic. This time she didn't look at me, didn't say that it was an accident (though it *was*), but held her injured hand with the other one, and made a valiant effort not to cry. I couldn't help seeing the tears in her eyes, though. And I

29

knew how much it had to hurt. Sam had slammed a car door on my hand once.

"There's a walk-in clinic," Dad started, but she shook her head.

"No. They can't do anything about it. I don't think anything's broken."

"Ice," I said, sounding strangled. "Put some ice on it. That helped me one time."

"Yes, ice," Crystal agreed. There wasn't any left in our thermos jug, so Dad ran and got some from some other picnickers who had an ice chest. He wrapped it in his clean handkerchief and she held it over her purple fingers, which I could see between the front seats from where I was cringing in regret.

She didn't get out of the car when Dad let us kids out at home. I hesitated on the sidewalk, looking in her own window. "I'm really sorry," I said inadequately.

She gave me a quick glance, then looked down at the hand in her lap. I could see the discoloration through the handkerchief, where it wasn't completely covered in ice. "Thank you," she said, in that small, soft voice.

"I'll get you home before that all melts," Dad said, and pulled away from the curb.

We walked into the house, carrying the depleted supplies.

"I'll never be friends with her now," I said dolefully, though that hadn't been high on my list of priorities. "I'll bet she hates me."

"Probably," Bonnie said.

Somehow, that didn't make me feel any better.

3

"It was not exactly an auspicious introduction," Dad said at the breakfast table Sunday morning, "but it's going to get better. Crystal's going to church with us today."

"I'm surprised she's agreed to get within a mile of us. At least within a mile of Nikki," Bonnie said.

Hurt, I couldn't believe she'd said that. "I didn't do anything on purpose. I'm really, really sorry, Dad!"

"I know that. Crystal knows that. Accidents happen. However"—and he looked right at me then—"there aren't going to be any more of them. Are there?"

I swallowed. "I hope not," I muttered.

"You can do better than that, Nicole," he said. He

never calls me that unless he's furious with me. When he reaches the ultimate—as after I spilled ink on some important papers on his desk—it becomes *Nicole Lorraine Simons*. "You will be walking on eggs from here on out, understood?"

"Understood," I echoed, and this time I had sense enough not to mutter.

So we went to church, and I stayed as far away from Crystal as it was possible to get.

She was wearing a pale blue suit that brought out the color of her eyes, and she looked very nice. Except for the bandage on her left hand with the purple fingers sticking out beyond the edge of the sling.

I stared at it in horror, but couldn't apologize again. Not that she didn't deserve it, but my voice wouldn't work.

Dad introduced her to everyone after the service. The pastor was delighted to hear that they were engaged, and sympathetic about her injury. "We were going shopping for an engagement ring this week," Dad said, "but it looks as if we'll have to wait until she can get a ring on that finger."

Standing well behind them in line as we went down the front steps, I continued to cringe. We'd gone to Saint Peter's ever since I was an infant, and Dad knew everybody. He made sure that Crystal met every one of them, and there wasn't a soul who didn't commiserate—usually with an appropriate facial expression—on the mangled hand.

Crystal was quiet and shy, but she did smile at most of them. She even made a small joke to Pastor Wylie when she commented that she'd really been looking forward to that engagement ring and wondered if she'd have to postpone the wedding until she could wear *that* ring.

He assured her, laughing, that a wedding could be worked around such an obstacle.

She never looked at me the entire time, and I wondered if she wanted me to feel as rotten as I felt. Spilling Jell-O on a washable shirt was bad enough, but crushing her hand in a car door went beyond anything even a sadist would have thought up. I hoped she believed that I hadn't intended any of it.

To our great relief, Dad and Crystal went off to dinner by themselves after we got home.

"They're talking about a wedding," I said to Bonnie while we were eating the BLTs that were *our* dinner. "Do you think they'll have a big church wedding? Even though Dad's only been widowed such a short time?"

"It'll probably be up to Crystal, whatever she wants," Bonnie said, licking mayonnaise off the edge of her sandwich. "She's a first-time bride. That means she's entitled to a long white dress and all the trimmings, if she wants them."

I stopped chewing. "Do you think she'll ask us to be bridesmaids?"

"After what you did to her yesterday? Nikki, get real! Besides, a bride usually asks her best friends to be her attendants. Sam, stop dripping all over your front! Use your napkin! And don't feed Buster from the table."

We talked about Crystal off and on, of course. How could we not, when Dad kept bringing up her name, and announcing their plans? After all the distress I'd caused her, no matter how inadvertent, I backed off as much as I could on criticism. When she came to the house, I tried to retreat to my room, or go out in the yard, or make an emergency trip to the library.

"Is she going to live here with us?" Sam asked, frowning slightly.

"Yes, of course," Dad said. "Married people usually live together in the same house."

"Where's she going to sleep?"

"In my room, naturally. That's customary too."

"Won't she mind sleeping in the same bed where Mom died?" It was Bonnie who asked that, very quietly and soberly.

Dad gave her a considering look. "We're getting a new bed. A king-sized one."

35

"Good thinking," Bonnie approved. "She might want to redecorate that room before the wedding."

Dan considered some more. "You really think so?"

"Ask her," Bonnie suggested.

And so before the new bed was moved in and set up, someone was hired to come in and paper and paint the master bedroom. "I'd do it myself," Crystal said apologetically, "if I had the use of both hands."

"No problem," Dad said. "Just let us know what you want done, and we'll do it."

I found out she'd had to go to the doctor, after all, and get pain medication so her hand wouldn't ache so bad that she couldn't work. One more thing for me to feel guilty about.

Finally Dad announced the wedding date: the week after school was out, just before Bonnie was leaving on a trip to build houses in Mexico with a group of kids from our community outreach program. "It'll be in our church," he told us.

Again, it was Bonnie who had an idea about how things were usually done. "She doesn't want to be married in her own church?"

"Crystal's never found a church home since she moved to Seattle," Dad said glibly. "So we'll do it at Saint Peter's."

"Will her family be coming? Will we need to give up

our bedrooms and sleep in sleeping bags on the back porch?"

"I don't believe she has any family to speak of. Nobody will be staying here except our own relatives, and Grandpa and Grandma don't like twin beds, so I think they've opted for a motel. We're going to cater the reception in the church hall, so you won't have to do anything about food."

It was a beautiful wedding, everybody said. If anyone but me thought it was too soon after Mama died, they didn't say so in my hearing. I did hear Grandma Booker commenting that poor Jeff was so lonely, it was a miracle he'd found Crystal, and she hoped they'd be very happy.

Afterward, though, when they'd gone off on the *Princess Marguerite* to Victoria, B.C., for a three-day honeymoon, I talked to Bonnie before we went to sleep. Grandma Simons was staying with us until Dad and Crystal got back, though we'd insisted that wasn't necessary.

"Didn't you think it was a peculiar wedding?" I asked into the darkened room.

"Crystal looked very nice—her gown was beautiful—and Dad looked pretty sharp, too," Bonnie said.

"I don't mean how they looked. I mean—didn't it

strike you as odd that she didn't have anybody there? All the guests were our relatives. Our friends. Dad's friends."

"Didn't she say none of her family are still alive?"

"Even her adopted parents? I remember her mother and father died in an accident when she was seven, but what about the rest of her relatives? Look how many we've got. Grandparents and aunts and uncles and cousins."

"Not everybody has a lot of relatives," Bonnie said sleepily. "Or maybe the ones she still has live a long way away. Anyway, Dad said she didn't have any family to speak of, didn't he?"

"What about friends? She didn't even have a friend. Her maid of honor was Dad's secretary, for Pete's sake. Didn't he say he'd met her three or four months ago, so she must have been living in Seattle at least that long. How could she not have any friends to invite to her wedding?"

"Hmm. I don't know," Bonnie said. "It does seem odd. I guess we can't ask her without being rude. Nikki, can I borrow that red blouse of yours, the one with no sleeves, to wear in Mexico?"

"I guess so. I'm going to get it back before you leave for D.C., right?"

"Right," my sister agreed, and that was the last chance

we got to discuss the wedding. But I thought about it, off and on, and wondered. It didn't seem normal for Crystal not to have either family or friends, somewhere.

Bonnie left on the bus with the other Youth Group kids. Dad and Crystal came home, and it was different from when Mom was alive.

The master bedroom looked very changed from when Mama was in it, when I'd spent so much time sitting on her bed with her, reading or poring over travel brochures or just talking.

I'd only peeked into it when nobody else was home. Three walls were pale lavender, and the fourth was papered in a floral pattern that was mostly purple. The king-sized bed had a white crocheted spread over a deeper purple coverlet. Crystal had taken down the blinds in favor of white draperies that she mostly kept wide open so that the room was filled with sunshine.

There was a drawing table situated where the light would fall fully on it in the morning, and some new shelves and storage areas where she'd moved in paints and artist supplies.

I was curious to know if she was any good as an artist, but I didn't go in and poke around to look at any of her stuff. I supposed she must be good or B&B wouldn't have hired her to illustrate any of their books.

B&B was Billock & Brandbury Books. Dad had worked for them for years, and he liked his job as an editorial director. It wasn't just a desk job. It wasn't as big a publishing house as the ones in New York, but besides working in the Seattle office he got to travel quite a bit. Before Mom got sick, she would sometimes go with him to places like Atlanta, or Honolulu, or Anchorage. I wondered if Crystal would travel with him, too, and if they'd insist that Sam and I have a baby-sitter while they were gone. We liked both our grandmothers, but they were sort of picky about what we did and how we ate, and they both had busy lives of their own.

I found out the first morning that Crystal had some different habits from the rest of us. She had brought a juicer with her, and she had fresh carrot juice for breakfast.

"That's all?" Sam asked, incredulous.

"I'll have some fruit later," she said, and sat watching the rest of us with our waffles and cereal.

"I'll call if I'm going to be late for dinner," Dad said, swiping up the last of his syrup. "What are your plans for today, sweetheart? Working on the Donniger drawings?"

"Yes, I think so. You want me to have dinner ready at six-thirty?"

She flicked a glance at me, then quickly away, which

I interpreted as meaning even as a non-cook she'd probably put together a better meal than I would. Okay by me, I thought.

Dad immediately disabused me of that notion. "You give her a hand, Nikki. Whatever help she needs."

"Sure," I said. He hadn't given me any specific orders for the day, so I decided I'd try to reestablish contact with some of my former friends, see what might be possible to plan for the summer.

Dad kissed her good-bye, and that hurt, too. Did she know she was sitting where Mom used to sit when she could still join us for meals? How did it feel to move into another woman's house, another woman's room, even with a different bed, and take over someone else's family?

I would have been pretty uncomfortable with that scenario, I decided.

I couldn't tell if Crystal was uncomfortable or not. She rinsed out her carrot juice glass and stuck it in the dishwasher. "Does everyone meet for lunch at noon?" she asked.

What was lunch if breakfast was carrot juice? "Uh . . . well, for the past year or so, everybody has fended for himself for lunch. Each one just gets whatever he wants, somewhere around noon. And cleans up after himself. If Dad's home, usually somebody waits on him."

Crystal nodded. "Sounds like a good plan. I'll be working upstairs, then."

I got on the phone as soon as she was gone and started calling kids I used to run around with. Joanna was willing to go to the pool that afternoon, but she was leaving the next day to visit her grandparents in Montana for a month. Scratch Joanna for a summer companion.

Ivy had a houseful of cousins that week, and another batch coming right after they left. Scratch Ivy.

Nobody was home at Nola's. Try again later. Tiffani was going with her mother to pick strawberries out in Marysville, and when they came home they were going to make jam. Did I want to help?

Cleaning berries didn't sound too intriguing. I made another couple of futile calls and decided I'd just go to the library and stock up on my summer reading.

Sam disappeared right after breakfast, without telling me where he was going. I made a mental note to remind him that he was supposed to do that, though I didn't really care where he went. He had lots of buddies and they'd probably ride bikes or go for a swim at the Y or get up a sandlot game.

I came home with an armload of books and carried them upstairs, then sneaked down and made a sandwich and got an apple to go with it, just before noon. I met Crystal coming down for her lunch and murmured

42

something about eating in my room, grateful that I didn't have to sit across the table from her and try to make conversation all by myself.

Maybe she felt the same way. I saw her go past my door with her own lunch on a tray, carrying it into the room that was now as much studio as bedroom.

I stayed up there reading most of the day, almost forgetting to come down and help with dinner. Crystal was just putting a big pan of lasagna into the oven, and had salad fixings on the counter. "You want to set the table? I thought maybe in the dining room would be nice."

We'd all moved into the kitchen when Mom had stopped joining us. "Okay," I said, and even got out the good dishes and made the table look nice.

Dad came in at twenty-five to seven. "Traffic was horrible," he announced, dropping his briefcase on the hall table. "Did you know Seattle gridlock is the worst in the country?"

Crystal came to meet him, lifting her face for a kiss. How long was it going to take me to keep from flinching every time he did that? *Of course he's going to kiss her,* Bonnie had said. *She's his new bride.* But I couldn't help turning away, unable to watch.

"Anything good in the mail?" Dad asked.

"Mail," Crystal said uncertainly. "Was I supposed to do something about collecting mail?"

"Nikki usually gets it. It comes just before noon." He looked at me.

"I forgot. I'll get it now," I said, and moved quickly to the mailbox beside the front door.

There was a handful of letters, including one for Miss Crystal Fontana, forwarded from her apartment in the city. I handed it all to Dad and he picked that one out, right off the top. "You've got something here from a lawyer's office in Eureka, California. They catching up to you with all those unpaid parking tickets?"

Crystal didn't laugh. In fact, I thought she lost a little color. She didn't even reach out a hand to take the letter.

"Want me to open it and see what they're nailing you for?" Dad asked, not noticing anything amiss. I wasn't positive I was catching anything, either, but I thought I was.

When she didn't reply, simply stood there with parted lips and a wooden expression, Dad slit the envelope and scanned the single enclosed sheet.

"Hey! What about this! You're an heiress, sweetheart! You didn't tell me you had any rich relatives!"

By this time I was convinced she really had gone pale. She still didn't reach for the letter.

"'This is to inform you that you are the principal beneficiary of the late Edna Milan of Trinidad, California'—isn't that a little town on the coast, just north of

Eureka?—'which consists primarily of a house at' . . . a house! On the coast. Hey, I knew I was getting a pearl, but I didn't realize you'd come with a bonus. You weren't really close to this aunt, were you?"

"No," she said stolidly.

I couldn't believe he didn't notice how she was reacting. Or, rather, not reacting. She might have been a post for all that she revealed of how she felt about this. I wondered if I should offer my sympathy, but I hesitated.

"They want you to contact them regarding this legacy. It's too late to do it today, but you can call them first thing in the morning." Dad put the letter and the rest of the mail, which had not excited his interest, on top of his briefcase. "Boy, am I hungry. I didn't have time for lunch today. Old Brandbury came in a few minutes after noon and wanted to talk about the new Adrian book, and by the time we'd finished, my one o'clock appointment was in. What do I smell? Lasagna?"

With his arm around her, they walked toward the kitchen.

The letter, wide open in plain sight, drew my attention.

If somebody left me an estate—a house—I'd have wanted to look at the letter myself. I'd have been excited.

Instead of that, it seemed more as if Crystal was . . . scared.

.

Yes, that was the impression I had. She was scared.

I read through the typed words and tried to figure out what there could be about them to frighten anybody.

Uneasily, I walked out to the kitchen to help carry in the food, and wondered if my imagination was running away with me again.

I wished Bonnie hadn't gone to Mexico, so I could talk to her about it. Or Mama. She'd never ridiculed anything I said, no matter how far out it was.

But of course if Mama had been there, Crystal wouldn't have been, and we'd never have heard of her inheritance.

"Here, let me carry that. It's heavy and hot," Dad said cheerfully as Crystal took the pan out of the oven.

And all through dinner I kept seeing the words from the lawyer on that single sheet of paper and wondering what about them had caused such a peculiar reaction.

The wedding had been peculiar, and so was this. No matter what anybody said, there was something different and strange about Crystal. How could Dad not be aware of it?

Dad was so busy talking about various deals and business arrangements that he didn't even notice that neither Crystal nor I said two words through the entire meal.

4

It was strange waking up alone in our bedroom, without Bonnie.

She had taken her laptop, so I could e-mail her, but she wouldn't always be able to plug in so she'd get my messages. Still, e-mail was better than nothing, even if all I said was, "I miss you, and you've only been gone two days! Speak to me!"

I didn't know if she got the messages or not. I didn't hear from her, and pictured her having so much fun with her friends that she didn't think to check for e-mail.

It was strange having a stepmother in the house. There was no way I could think of her as a *mother*. She tried to stay out of my way; she hardly came out of her room/studio except at mealtimes. Or maybe she really was too busy to come out and wasn't just doing it to avoid me. Most of the time I didn't even remember she was in the house.

The morning after she got the letter from the lawyer in California, we were all together having a late breakfast. Dad had stayed up half the night finishing a manuscript he wanted to discuss with his assistant that day, and so he hadn't left at the usual time. He gave Crystal a big smile and reminded her, "You're going to call that lawyer, what was his name? George Udall? See what this inheritance actually amounts to?"

Crystal stirred uneasily, swirling the carrot juice in her glass. "I'll call him later. I really want to get to that last sketch this morning."

For once, Dad sensed her resistance. "You're not intimidated about it, are you? How difficult can it be, just to call him and give him your new name and address?"

"I could just write to him," Crystal said. "That would be easier."

"Easier than picking up the phone and dialing?" Dad wrote lots of letters, but he also made lots of phone calls because, he said, you got an immediate response to your questions. "Listen, sweetie, if it bothers you, I'll do it. Okay? Nikki, bring me the phone, please."

Crystal was making tiny protesting sounds, but not enough to stop Dad. He got through to the attorney in California and conveyed the necessary information, then asked, "What is this place, exactly? You mentioned a house."

Crystal was definitely fidgeting, moving her glass in wet circles, crossing and uncrossing her legs.

Dad gave the man time to reply, then grinned. "Sounds interesting. You want to talk directly to my wife? Here she is."

He handed over the phone with an encouraging smile. "Big house, near the coast. Just reaffirm who you are."

Crystal accepted the phone as if it were a snake, I observed. Why? I hadn't seen her using the phone much since she'd come, but it couldn't be that much of a big deal. I mean, what's to be afraid of in a phone?

"This is Crystal Fontana. Only it's Crystal Simons, now. My husband gave you my new address." After a moment, she thanked him, and handed the phone back to me to replace on its cradle.

"There," Dad said. "He'll be in touch. Well, I'd better run. See you tonight, everybody." I guessed he thought he'd made something easier for her, but I wasn't sure he had.

He tousled Sam's hair, patted my shoulder, and bent to kiss Crystal. I supposed I'd eventually get used to it, but it continued to bother me. It was almost as if Mom were still upstairs, sick in bed, and Dad was in the kitchen smooching somebody else.

It was strange to have all the time I wanted to read, and to have no school assignments. After about a week, I needed something more.

"Aren't we going to take a vacation this summer, Dad?" I finally asked. We were at the dinner table—we were eating all meals in the dining room these days—because that was practically the only time I saw him.

"Vacation? Nikki, I brought home two full-length manuscripts to read tonight, and I won't get through both of them," he said.

"Why don't you read them at the office?" Sam asked innocently.

"Because at the office there are always people coming in and out and needing my opinion and consultations, that's why. There's not enough time at the office."

"We used to take vacations," Sam said. "I liked Disneyland. And Copalis Beach."

Unexpectedly, Crystal made a contribution. "I used to love the beach when I was Sam's age."

"We all love the beach," I said. "Maybe for just a weekend, Dad?"

"I don't know. We'll have to see how things go. Listen, I have to run up to Marysville on the way home.

What do you say I pick up some fresh strawberries and we have shortcake for supper?"

There was a murmur of approval, and we each went our separate ways for the day.

I came into the kitchen in the middle of the afternoon and found Crystal there studying a cookbook. She flushed a little, as if there were something to feel embarrassed about. "I defrosted pork chops, but I never cooked any before," she admitted. She was wearing shorts and a tank top, and she looked about seventeen. Younger than Bonnie.

"I think they're easy," I said. "Mom sometimes just baked them. In the oven, not the microwave. With baked potatoes or yams. Or you can fry them in that big non-stick pan, and braise potatoes in with them. Or make mashed potatoes. Or—"

"Enough, enough! Baking should be easy. For how long?"

She leafed through the pages until she came to that information, because I didn't remember.

"With a salad, and strawberry shortcake, that should do it, shouldn't it?"

She looked pleased to have figured out a menu. I felt a twinge of sympathy. Since Bonnie had left, I felt pretty inadequate in that department.

I'd finally made connections with a friend to go

swimming at the Y, and I was late getting home. Even Dad beat me, so I washed up quickly and slipped into my place just in time for saying grace.

The pork chops and the baked potatoes came out great. She'd made a salad with avocados and cashews in addition to the regular stuff, and it was super. Everybody said so, and Crystal flushed with pleasure at the triumph.

And then she brought in the shortcake.

It had strawberries, all right. If I'd been home to clean them, I'd have been in the kitchen when she made the cake. Real cake. I would have told her.

It looked delicious. But the minute he took the first bite, Sam blurted out, "This isn't shortcake! Not like Mom's!"

The satisfaction slid off Crystal's face as she stared down at her dish in bewilderment.

I tested my own dessert and discovered plain old yellow cake.

"What did I do wrong?" Crystal asked in that soft, breathy little voice.

Dad took a big bite. "Oh, don't sweat it, sweetie. Pam always made shortcake with biscuits. That's just what we're used to. But this is fine. Delicious, in fact. I hope there's enough for seconds. I don't usually approve of seconds on dessert, but since we only have fresh strawberries for a few weeks out of the year, this is an exception."

Maybe he was too effusive. I murmured appreciation, too, but it wasn't enough. Crystal remained crushed, though she didn't say any more. Her perfect dinner was spoiled.

And it wasn't as if it didn't all taste good. It was simply different from what we were used to.

It occurred to me that there were going to be a lot of moments like this. She had no way of knowing how Mom had done things. And she was never going to *be* Mom; she had to be herself and find her own ways, and we'd have to get used to them.

I realized I didn't really want her to be hurt every time she tried something on her own. I knew too well what that felt like to want to inflict it on anyone else.

Maybe more to change the subject than for any other reason, Dad said, "You know, I've been thinking about what you all said about the beach. I do have a heavy schedule lined up, and I don't think the bank account is all that healthy, after catering the wedding and everything—"

Another slam at Crystal, in an oblique way, though of course it had been his wedding expense as well as hers. I glanced at her and saw that though I knew he hadn't meant it that way, she caught it, the same as I did. At least he hadn't mentioned that he'd used some of the money we'd saved up to go to Europe before we knew Mom was dying.

"Well, it occurred to me. There's that house you inherited, sweetie. I think that lawyer indicated it's on the beach, or near the beach, or something. Northern California's not so far away so I could drive back and forth on weekends, at least, and probably load up a bunch of work to do down there during the week. And it wouldn't cost anything to stay there, so the expense would be no object. What do you think?"

He was looking at us kids, not at Crystal. Sam immediately began to bounce up and down in his seat. "Could I take Jeremy with me, Dad? So there'd be somebody I know to do things with? Huh? Could I?"

Dad should have been looking at his new wife. I didn't think he knew her well enough to pick up on all the nuances in her posture and her expression, but I thought I was learning, though I had no idea why she reacted the way she did.

We knew she was shy. He'd told us that before he married her. She felt insecure about a lot of things, particularly in personal relationships. Frankly, I was surprised he'd been able to talk her into marrying him.

And now she was stricken dumb, or almost.

"Don't you think that would solve the vacation problem?" He did look at her now, and he still wasn't seeing what I was seeing: a woman frozen in dismay, though I couldn't imagine why.

She'd forgotten to eat, though the shortcake really was pretty good. "I . . . don't think I could take a vacation right now," she almost whispered. "I have all those . . . drawings to finish."

"Do the same thing I'm going to do," Dad urged. "Take the work with you. You can draw or paint or whatever you're going to do in California as well as here. You work at home, anyway. If we have to come back to Seattle a time or two for consultations or to deliver something, we can do that. What do you think, Nikki? You want a beach vacation?"

I'd never turned down an opportunity to go to the beach in my life. Yet I hesitated, uncertain as to why Crystal didn't want to go. She'd just said she had always enjoyed beaches.

"Have you been there?" I asked her, rather than replying to Dad. "Do you know what the house is like?"

"The lawyer said her aunt lived in it until she died a few months ago. It's completely furnished, electricity still on, phone installed. Not that that matters; we've got a cell phone that's good anywhere. All we'd need to do is buy groceries, and there are probably some of those still left in the house. It's ready to move into," Dad said. "Is this the aunt you lived with after your parents were killed, sweetie?"

He'd fallen into the habit of shortening *sweetheart* to *sweetie,* and I found myself gritting my teeth every time he said it. What did you do if your new husband did something that made you want to scream? Well, maybe it didn't affect Crystal that way, but something was sure out of whack here.

"Sweetie?" Dad prompted, and it took all my will-power not to kick him under the table.

Crystal licked her lips. "Yes, that was Aunt Edna."

"So is this the house where you lived when you were a child?"

She had sort of hunched in on herself, as if she were cold. "I was only there for a short time. It was a long time ago."

"But you must remember the house," Dad said. "Big place, the lawyer said."

"Yes. I think there are . . . six or eight bedrooms." She shut her eyes briefly, almost wincing, and I had a sudden intuitive conviction that she'd slept alone in one of them, seven years old and having just lost her parents, and that she'd been afraid.

Was that it? She had bad memories of the house, and was reluctant to go back there?

"Plenty big enough for the four of us. And for Sam

to take a friend along if he wants to. Big house, no rent, a beach. Is it a good beach?"

"Good" to Dad meant miles and miles of sand, maybe some rocky outcroppings, driftwood and starfish and shells. Mom had collected shells. And no people, or as few as possible.

Crystal seemed to be floundering, moving her lips without speech, her fingers twitching until she put them down in her lap, out of sight. "It . . . it seemed quite a way, when I was seven. I was never allowed to go down there alone."

"Of course not, at seven," Dad agreed.

"Aunt . . . Edna didn't really care for beaches," Crystal said, as if compelled by the strength of Dad's personality to produce answers no matter how much she'd rather not have done it.

"But the house overlooks the ocean, doesn't it? On a cliff, I think he said. But there's a path down to the beach?"

"Stairs," Crystal said. "A lot of stairs."

"Well, we're all young and healthy. I wouldn't even miss my workouts at the Y if I was climbing stairs every day. And it would take the edge off some of Sam's energy, which would be a blessing to all of us." He smiled at my little brother. "Let me see what I can work out at the office. Let's plan on loading up the old van and heading for California!"

Crystal visibly gathered her resolution. "I . . . don't think that's a good idea, Jeff. Not now. Maybe . . . later."

"But now's when the kids have the vacation time, right? And June and July are about the best times of the year for weather. If I remember correctly, it may be chilly enough even then, so we'll need to take jackets. I think I'll try to get the van in for servicing tomorrow, so we'll be ready to take off."

I couldn't believe how obtuse he was being. Crystal clearly did not want to go. My guess was not now, not ever, though she'd said maybe later. How could he be crazy in love with her and not be picking up the signals she was giving off?

Granted, she was a lot more subtle than Mom had been. Mom would just have spoken up in very plain language and made him listen, made him understand, and Crystal hadn't yet learned that that was what worked with Dad. Once he has this great idea implanted in his mind, you might have to smack him alongside the head to get his attention long enough to get across to him that there is another perspective than his own.

"That was delicious, sweetie. I wasn't kidding about the seconds. Is there enough to go around again?"

Crystal didn't move. She sat there with her own shortcake practically untouched, as if she'd been turned to stone. After a few seconds, I stood up and reached for Dad's bowl. "I'll get it. I think I'll have some more too."

"Me three!" Sam announced, getting up to follow me.

I wondered if Crystal would try to communicate once we'd left the room, but as far as I could tell, she didn't. Dad was off on something about a client they both knew, and he was so used to her being quiet that he didn't even notice that this was a different kind of silence.

No wonder Mom had sometimes—before she got sick—been so emphatic. It was the only way to live with Dad and survive. My sympathies were definitely turning toward Crystal.

I don't know what she said to him in private, if she said anything at all. When we were all together, I know she tried, in complete futility, to convey to Dad that she'd rather stay home and finish her work here. He knew that technically she could work anywhere, and he was all fired up about inspecting the house she had inherited.

There were projects he could take with him to work on in California. He would always be available to the office by phone. Sam was ecstatic; Jeremy's parents had said he could go along.

I had no idea why Crystal didn't want to go, but I was sure she didn't. And I couldn't understand why Dad was treating her as if she were one of us kids, not a wife whose input was as important as his own. If it really mattered to her, why didn't she fight harder? Even though I'd gotten enough clues to realize fighting wasn't her style, I didn't quite have the nerve to point out to Dad that he didn't have to make all the decisions without her.

None of my somewhat estranged friends was free to go to keep me company. I wanted to go—it sounded intriguing, a beach down a long flight of stairs, right on the ocean, and a house that might prove interesting, too. Certainly different from the one I'd lived in all my life.

I got up the courage to ask her. "Eureka's the town that has all the houses built in the eighteen eighties, isn't it?"

"Yes. It has the Carson mansion, the most photographed house in the country, and a walking historical tour of some of the others."

"Is your aunt's house—your house—very old?"

"Built in 1902, I think," she said.

It didn't occur to me until later, and then I thought I was probably mistaken, but wasn't that an odd thing for a seven-year-old to have noted, the year a house had been built? Or had she been there since then?

"No," she said softly when I asked. "I never went back."

"Your adoptive parents took you away, then."

"Yes. Far away."

There was something in the way she said that, too, that piqued my curiosity. Far away, so that she'd never gone back. Far away—not just from the house, but from whatever had happened to her there?

I was hesitant, but I had to know. "Was your aunt—abusive? Is that why you were taken away from her and put up for adoption?"

For a moment, something twisted in her face. Revulsion? Shock? "Oh, no, she was good to me. But she thought I'd be better off in a family, with a mother and a father instead of an old aunt."

"So where did you live, then, after you were adopted?"

"In Portland," she said, busy folding laundry.

Portland? But that was only a three- or four-hour drive from here, and maybe double that from Eureka. "Are they dead now, then?"

"No, they're both alive, though not well. They're . . . older," she said, and I had the feeling she wasn't really thinking about what I was asking.

Then why didn't they come to your wedding?

That was a question I *couldn't* ask, though. Nor why she didn't want to go to Trinidad, near Eureka. And I couldn't tell her to stand up to my dad and make him listen, really *hear* what she was saying, though I wanted to.

I was more and more eager to go to that old house near the beach. I hoped there was a library nearby, because I wouldn't know anybody there to pal around with, and nobody else would have any time to spend with me. I could enjoy myself alone on a beach, however, especially if there were books for the quiet times.

I looked forward to a vacation away from home. When Dad said, "We're leaving Saturday, start packing!" I packed.

But I knew Crystal didn't want to go, and her reluctance created an uneasiness in the back of my mind that would, before the vacation was over, become fully justified.

She was an adult, I told myself. She was married to my father, and she ought to be grown up enough not to let him bully her—however tenderly he did it!—and I couldn't control any of his decisions, anyway, so I might as well relax and enjoy it.

So, of course, we went to Trinidad.

5

We got a late start because Crystal said she wasn't feeling well. "Why don't you just take the kids and go without me?" she said. "You'll all have a good time and I'll rest and get a lot of work done when I feel better."

Dad was crushed. "You want me to leave you alone when we're still practically honeymooning? Sweetie, don't be absurd!"

"I really don't feel up to driving all that way right now," Crystal said, as forcefully as I'd ever heard her up to this point.

He put a hand on her head. "Running a fever? No? Upset stomach? Maybe we should see a doctor."

She brushed his hand aside. "It's nothing that won't pass in a few hours," she said. "Just go, honey, please."

"If it'll pass in a few hours, we'll wait," Dad said. "I'll get my briefcase and see what I can accomplish until you feel better. Why don't you go up and lie down for an hour or so?"

I wished I could read behind the unsmiling face when she said, in that soft voice, "I don't think that's going to help enough, Jeff."

"The kids and I will all be quiet. Why don't we see what an hour lying down will do?" Dad said.

An hour later, when he sent me upstairs to check on her, Crystal was not lying down. She was sitting on the edge of the bed, her face wooden when I peeked in the open doorway.

"Are you any better?" I asked.

She sounded like one of those mechanical dolls that you can program to speak. I saw her swallow before she replied. "I don't think it's going to matter, no matter how long I rest. I might just as well go downstairs and we can leave."

Dad gave her an enthusiastic hug, as if she'd reported full recovery, and in five minutes we were backing out onto the street.

The drive was too far to do in one day, though Dad might have done it if he'd been alone. But not with a wife and three kids and a dog along. So we stopped overnight in Grants Pass. Dad was in a good mood, willing to stop at fast-food places he ordinarily would have scorned, hitting the rest stops as soon as anyone mentioned needing one, making sure old Buster got in his exercise, and pit stops as well.

Dad drove fast, but he's a good driver and I enjoyed it.

Crystal may have been nervous, but I don't believe it had anything to do with Dad's driving or the traffic down I-5. Dad kept trying to make her laugh, telling stories, jokes, singing.

Nothing actually thawed her out. Not that she was being nasty or uncooperative; she was just subdued. Not into singing "One Hundred Bottles of Beer on the Wall." Not up to bothering to come up with entertainments of her own.

Sam and Jeremy made enough noise between them to cover any lack of it from anyone else. At the motel where we stopped for the night, the boys had a room to themselves, with Buster, and I got one alone, too. It was the first time I'd ever been in a motel without Bonnie. I thought wistfully of all the fun she was undoubtedly having with the other kids on the missionary bus, and of the houses they'd be building for poor people in Mexico.

After having a sister to talk to before you went to sleep every night, for your whole life, it was a big adjustment to make. I speculated on what Dad and Crystal were talking about in the next room, and I sort of understood why he said he needed a wife again so soon. Even if it was only to have someone to talk to.

But I'd have bet she wasn't telling him why she didn't want to return to that house where she'd lived for a few months when she was only seven.

Why not? Weren't you supposed to trust the person you were married to?

I wish you were here, Bonnie. You're smarter than I am. Older, at least. I'm sort of getting to know how to deal with having a stepmother. Crystal isn't so bad; she just doesn't know how we do things, and we don't know how she wants to do them. I'm willing to try.

Only I don't know how. Dad ought to be figuring out things, only he isn't doing it. He doesn't even see that there is anything he needs to figure out.

But Crystal is scared of something. Intimidated by something. And she doesn't know what to do, either. Maybe if you were here, we could put our brains together and make sense of it.

Because, I admitted to myself, *it's beginning to scare me.*

We didn't go all the way into Eureka. Trinidad is a little tiny town—maybe you'd call it a village—perched on the bluffs high above the Pacific a few miles up the coast. There was a modern-looking supermarket and, I noticed with delight, a small library. We made a loop through the charming little houses and looked down over the boat basin, hemmed in by volcanic black, rocky projections. It was so charming that it sent prickles up my spine in anticipation of spending some time here. Dad had called Mr. Udall, the lawyer, and gotten directions to the house because Crystal said she didn't remember how to get to it.

Although she'd said the house had been built in 1902, and the houses I'd seen pictures of in Eureka and south of there in Ferndale had all been constructed in the mid-to-late 1800s, I was sort of expecting a Victorian mansion.

It was nothing so grand as those. To reach it, we took a side road through imposing trees that closed over our heads, leaving us in virtual darkness even in mid-afternoon. And then we came out of the towering giants into a graveled drive, and we could see and smell the ocean.

The house was large and undistinguished except for a wide, covered veranda that ran around three sides of it. There was a single detached garage on the woods side, where we parked the car.

Everybody piled out, except Crystal. Buster trotted

around, smelling everything and watering the un-kempt grass and flower beds.

"Wow!" Sam said, and ran toward the top of the stairway, marked by heavy wooden posts.

"Hey!" Dad shouted. "Come back here! No explor-ing on your own until I've had a look around, okay? Stick together until I know what we're dealing with." He turned, halfway to the nearest set of steps to the porch, and looked back at the car. "Come on, sweetie, aren't you going to get out?"

I was closer to her, and I saw how badly she did *not* want to follow the rest of us.

Why? What had happened in this house that had her paralyzed with fear? How could she come here, if my speculations were accurate, without telling Dad why this was so impossible for her to do?

Yet when he walked back and opened her door, and took hold of her hand, she came docilely enough.

"It's big, all right," Dad was saying with satisfaction. "Old-fashioned, but well built, from what I can judge. Needs a coat of paint. Paint doesn't wear well here where the salt air blows against it all the time. Scours it right down to the bare boards."

"Dad," Sam called out, "it's just a whole bunch of steps and a winding path down to the bottom. Nothing dangerous—there're railings in most places. Can't we go down?"

"Not until I say so. Come help haul stuff into the kitchen. We'll be needing a meal before long, and all our meat and produce is in the back of the van. Make yourself useful."

There had been time enough for Dad to get a set of keys in the mail, and he flipped through them until he found one that unlocked the door into the kitchen. It was big and semimodern. That meant a wood range, alongside an electric one, which drew the boys' attention.

"Two stoves," Sam said. "How come?"

"The woodstove was probably put in when the house was built," Crystal said. "They would have kept it even after they had electricity, because the power goes out sometimes."

To my astonishment, she had walked right into the house along with the rest of us, even letting go of Dad's hand. And even more baffling, the distress she had worn like a cloak from the time we left home—no, before that—seemed to have fallen away, leaving her the way she'd been before the letter had come from Mr. Udall.

The boys lugged in boxes and grocery bags. Crystal opened the refrigerator, which had been left running, and began to put vegetables away, and meat packages. Buster kept getting in the way so that people had to dodge around him until Dad ordered him to stay on the rag rug just inside the door.

"I guess we'd better parcel out bedrooms and bring in our luggage next," Dad said. He put an arm around Crystal. "You going to come with us, sweetie, and tell us which rooms to take?"

"You can take any room you like. I thought we'd probably use the one that was Aunt Edna's, though it's at the back of the house. No view. But if you'd rather switch—"

"I don't care whether I have a view or not," Dad stated. "As long as I've got you as a roommate. Come on, troops, let's take a look at the rest of the place."

There was a big round table in the kitchen and I suspected that would be where we ate all our meals. The adjoining dining room had big, heavy, dark furniture, and didn't look as if anyone had used it since Franklin Roosevelt was president. Behind glass doors, fancy dishes were displayed, and I hoped Crystal wouldn't want to use them. Mom's idea of vacation eating was paper plates, and I'd noticed there was no dishwasher in the kitchen, though there had been a small microwave on one of the counters.

We crossed over a hallway that ran from the back to

the front of the house, into a double parlor. My interest was immediately caught by shelves of books in both sections. They weren't new, but maybe I wouldn't even need a library.

The furniture wasn't as old as the house, but it was worn and comfortable looking, most of it covered in flowered chintz. There were plenty of pillows, none of them matching, and a rocking chair facing a smallish TV. No recliner where Dad could put his feet up. In the back section of the parlor stood an old-fashioned organ with yellowing keys. I poked at it, and it responded in a halfhearted way.

"I guess maybe you have to pump it," Dad offered.

There was an enclosed room across the entire front of the house, overlooking the ocean, which was a gorgeous shade of blue in the late afternoon sun. It had wicker furniture, more chintz and pillows, and some plants struggling to survive.

Dad rapped his knuckles on the expanse of glass. "It's been modernized enough to put in double-paned windows. Should keep the winds from being lethal in the winter."

There was no porch furniture on the veranda. Aunt Edna had done her ocean-watching from inside the enclosed section of what might once have been part of the porch.

We tromped back out into the hall and discovered a utility room and pantry of sorts, with a reasonably modern set of laundry equipment. That was a relief. I'd begun to picture doing our washing by hand.

The boys raced ahead up the stairs. I trailed Dad and Crystal, whose reserve, if not vanished, had substantially diminished. I looked around as if I were that seven-year-old girl who had come here after her parents had died, seeing it as she would have seen it.

Would I have been terrified? Well, there was nothing in the house itself to scare me, but if I'd just lost my parents and was all alone in the world—except for an older aunt, whom I may or may not have already known—that would be frightening enough for anybody.

A part of me was disappointed, a little, in the house. Another—maybe larger?—part was relieved that this was not the haunted house I'd halfway been imagining.

The second floor had six bedrooms and two bathrooms. Dad gave a grunt of satisfaction on discovering the second one. "This one's mine and Crystal's," he announced. "You kids can share the other one."

Crystal seemed to be fine, now, and I began to doubt my earlier convictions about her reluctance to be here. Maybe Bonnie was right; I did read too many scary books and I was letting imagination run away with me.

Crystal opened a door into a room toward the rear side of the house. "This was Aunt Edna's room," she said, and stood aside for the rest of us to walk into it.

No Gothic horror. Just an ordinary bedroom, with a double bed, a big dresser with lots of drawers, a dressing table, a small case of more old books. There were hairbrushes and some small junk on top of the dresser.

Dad was looking at the bed. "Hmm. Looks small after ours, doesn't it? I wonder if we could get a king-sized delivered out here tomorrow?"

"Can we pick our own room?" Sam demanded. "Can we go look at the rest of them? Which one was yours, Crystal?"

"The one directly across the hall," she said, making no move to go look at it.

I went with the boys, though, leaving Dad and Crystal standing in the middle of their new bedroom. It was kind of embarrassing to be around them, if you know what I mean.

There was nothing to indicate that this room had ever belonged to a little girl. Of course that had been, what, over twenty years ago. And she probably hadn't slept there long enough to have had it redecorated or fixed up for her.

It had a four-poster bed (no canopy), and a rag rug

on a wood floor, and a rocking chair and a dresser. Plus there was a small writing desk. Jeremy pulled out the drawers and found they were all empty.

No lost letters, no hidden clues to anything, I thought, jeering silently at myself. Not like Nancy Drew at all.

"We'll keep this one," Sam announced. "Which one you going to take, Nikki?"

"It doesn't matter," I said. "Without Bonnie, they're all going to be just ordinary bedrooms. Maybe I'll have Buster move in with me, just to have somebody to talk to."

I knew, however, the moment I checked the last room at the end of the hall, on the side facing the ocean, that I'd found "my" room.

I could see the ocean, far below. Not the beach, just the water. What is there about water that is so magical? Mama always thought so too. Far out on the horizon was a smudge that was some sort of boat—or is it a ship when it's that big? Even as I stood there, entranced, a sailboat hove into view, much closer to land.

"I'll take this one," I said aloud, although there was no one there to hear me. I was so used to talking to Bonnie that it didn't seem natural to refrain from speaking. Even talking to a dog would be preferable to complete silence.

Aside from the view, which was spectacular, the room was as plain as the others. A double bed, a small desk, a rocking chair, another braided rag rug, somewhat faded but still colorful. A no-particular-pattern quilt on the bed, and a reading light on a stand beside it.

There was also a window seat, with padded cushions. A perfect place for reading, and when I wanted relief from the printed page I could raise my eyes and stare out at that fabulous ocean. It lived up to its name, today: Pacific. Calm, placid, except for a few slightly curling breakers as the currents or the tides reached for the shore that was hidden below me by the cliff with the stairs.

It had two closet doors. And me with my jeans, shorts, and tops, no more than what I could cram into one suitcase, which was the limit Dad had set. I checked out the first one, and set the wire hangers to jangling in the dusty interior.

Just for the heck of it, I rapped on the side walls. No hollow sounds. No secret passageways.

Grinning at myself, I stepped to the other door and opened it. And surprise! It was not a closet after all, but stairs, winding upward.

An attic! Maybe there was some old treasure in the attic. Trunks full of old letters, or romantic clothes from the 1930s, or *National Geographic*s with pictures of exotic places I'd probably never get to see except in a magazine.

Without hesitation, I started up the stairs. There was light coming from up above, so I wouldn't be in the dark. And I'd already given up on this being a haunted house with a mysterious past.

I emerged a moment later into a tower room with windows on all sides.

It wasn't large, and there was nothing in it but a faint layer of dust that showed my footsteps, and a binocular case on the floor. The view was so incredible, I caught my breath.

I'd been able to see the ocean from my room below, but this was much higher. I was above the trees, deep green spruce and pine and I thought I recognized a couple of redwoods. We had driven through magnificent stands of those giants for miles just north of here.

I picked up the binoculars and put them to my eyes. The sailboat had been joined by a second, and they raced toward the bay to the south. I watched them until they disappeared, then swung the glasses around and swept toward the north.

And stopped. There was a house, not too terribly far away, almost hidden in the forest. If it, too, had not had a tower, I probably couldn't have spotted it at all.

A Victorian mansion, just the kind I'd hoped *this* house would turn out to be.

It had a steep, sharply pointed roof on the tower, with windows on all sides like the tower I was standing in. Below it were more rooftops, enough to indicate a sizable house, much larger than this one. "A mansion," I breathed in satisfaction.

"Nikki? Where are you?"

I turned away from the window, but retained the binoculars. "Come on up, Daddy! It's a great view!"

He said something to Crystal, and apparently she declined to accompany him, though the boys clumped noisily behind him.

Their reactions didn't disappoint me. "Wow!" Sam said as he and Jeremy plastered their faces against the window facing most straight-on toward the ocean.

Dad looked around with delight. "Hey, this is really something. Let me see the glasses, honey." I handed them over and enjoyed his expression as he scoped everything out. When he had twisted to the north, he paused, as I had.

"We have a neighbor," I told him, as if he couldn't see it. "I'd sure like to see that house up close. It looks wonderful."

"Eureka's full of spectacular old houses. We can drive by some of them tomorrow when I go into town to find a bigger bed. Somebody's living in that one. I can see someone in one of the tower windows."

"Really? Let me see." He handed over the glasses and I brought them back into focus on the intriguing house. Sure enough, it did look as if someone in a blue shirt or blouse was moving behind the window. And then the blue was gone, and there was only a blank expanse of glass. "I'd sure like to see what it's like inside. A lot fancier than this house, I'll bet."

Be careful what you wish for, Mom used to say. *You might get it.*

Who would have dreamed what I'd get from such a simple wish?

b

"You want to come along and help me pick out a bed?" Dad asked, and for once he didn't call her by that irritating nickname.

Crystal, clearing off the breakfast table, shook her head. "No. You know what I like. Something as close as possible to what we have at home."

Dad was disappointed. "You sure? I thought I'd give the kids a quick historical tour of the old houses after I get the bed."

"No, thanks. I'd like to set up that corner bedroom as a studio, so I can get to work on those illustrations." She had her back to us so I couldn't see her face, but she sounded perfectly normal.

We'd all been really tired from the long drive, and had slept well. No visitations from ghosts, or strange noises in the night. Might as well give up on that interesting possibility, I thought. This house was a bust. Too ordinary, as ordinary as Aunt Edna apparently had been.

The rest of us were ready to go, though Sam and Jeremy weren't sure they were too fascinated with the idea of looking at old houses. They were more eager to go down to the beach.

"This afternoon," Dad promised. "After lunch. We'll be back by noon, sweetie."

He kissed her again before we left. Jeremy and Sam rolled their eyes and made faces at each other.

Buster stood by the back door and wagged his tail, but Dad shook his head. "Not this trip, fella. You stay here and keep Crystal company. Come on, gang, let's go get a new bed."

We went on out to the main road and headed for Eureka, the big city in Humboldt County. As we drove into town, we were close to the edge of the water, and Sam stared at it in dismay. "Is this what the beach is going to be like at our place?"

"No. That's out on the ocean, and there's a sandy beach, I'm sure. These are mudflats at low tide in the bay. Don't worry."

Dad picked out the bed by testing it himself, and

having me stretch out beside him, and the man agreed to have it delivered that afternoon. That hadn't taken very long, so we got a quick tour through Old Town, with its bricked streets and shops in colorful "old" new Victorian houses. Then we picked up a chamber of commerce brochure and followed the tour spelled out to show us the most attractive of the houses.

Most of them had been constructed in the 1800s, and many of those had recently been repainted and refurbished. I'd seen pictures of houses like these, but the boys hadn't, and even as reluctant as they'd been to waste time looking at buildings instead of being on the beach, they were impressed in spite of themselves.

"They're so tall," Jeremy breathed.

"And painted colors I've never seen on houses before," Sam said. "Look at that one—yellow and pale green and even lavender!"

"Most of them must have fourteen-foot ceilings on the ground floor, maybe ten-foot ceilings on the second floor. And attics almost that high. Must be the devil to heat in the wintertime," Dad said.

We crept along Hillsdale Street, only a few blocks long but lined with these magnificent old mansions from the lumbering days, when people thought the redwoods would last forever. It was almost like stepping back a hundred years into history.

"Crystal will be sorry she didn't come," Sam predicted, "when we tell her about these."

She wasn't, though. She smiled as we ate our sandwiches around the big kitchen table, with Buster waiting for surreptitiously dropped tidbits, and told her about the grand ladies of Victorian houses.

"I like a rather more modern house, myself," she observed quietly.

Like this one, with no dishwasher, I thought, knowing who'd be the one to do most of the dishes. So far, though, Crystal was going along with Mom's standard of using mostly paper plates.

"After all," she concurred when we suggested it, "this is supposed to be a vacation."

"Did you get your studio set up?" Dad asked, reaching for the mustard. "Need any help with the heavy stuff?"

"There isn't any heavy stuff," she told him. "I even got a little sketching done while you were gone."

"When are we going to see whatever you're drawing?" Sam asked, a rim of mayonnaise around his mouth.

Crystal hesitated, glancing at Dad. "These particular drawings aren't especially interesting. They're for a book on botany. Mosses, ferns, plants, that kind of thing."

"Show them to the kids," Dad said. "None of my kids can draw a straight line, so they ought to be impressed. I am."

"It must be your genes that made all of us such klutzes when it comes to drawing," Sam said, trying to get the mayonnaise with his tongue.

"And left all of us unable to carry a tune in a bucket," I added. I gave Crystal a look. "Not that it keeps any of us from singing when we travel."

She laughed. She seemed quite at ease, now, and I couldn't for the life of me figure out what was making the difference. Maybe she'd dreaded coming to this house because of bad memories—either of the house itself or of the time when she'd lost her family and had to come here—and once she got here she discovered that as an adult she could handle it now. That it no longer bothered her the way she'd thought it would.

The minute Sam wiped the last crumb off his chin, he was on his feet. "Now we go to the beach!"

Cleaning up was only a matter of dumping the paper plates and used napkins into the trash can, and wiping off the table. Even Crystal appeared willing to accompany us this time, and with Buster bounding ahead of us, we started down the steps.

There were a lot of them. In places, there were stretches of rocky or sandy path, and then more stairs, which doubled back on themselves a dozen times before we reached the bottom.

Long before we got there, we could see that it was a

genuine beach, wide and sandy and with dark outcroppings of rock sometimes reaching out into the foaming surf. The sound of it was mesmerizing, and the boys were rushing out into it before Dad yelled at them to back off.

"It isn't really safe to swim along this coast, in most places," Crystal said, raising her voice to be heard over the sounds of the sea. "There's too much of an undertow. I think there's a little bay a ways to the north where it's safer."

"No swimming here!" Dad bellowed, much to Sam's dismay. But the boys backed off, finally content simply to wade out to their knees. I soon found out why they settled for that much when I waded in myself.

"This is *cold!*" I said as my feet froze almost instantly.

Not being able to swim didn't spoil it, though. It was pale, clean sand, and there were small shells and all kinds of stuff washed up. I found a colored glass float, off a net, Dad thought, and Jeremy turned up a starfish.

Ahead of us, black rock protruded into the water and we started around it. Crystal called out a warning. "That may be covered when the tide comes in, so you can't come back that way, so don't go too far."

The boys stopped and stared at her. "How will we know how long it's safe to keep going?"

"We'll have to get a tide table." Dad said. "We can probably get one in Trinidad, or certainly in Eureka next time we go in."

I didn't want to get trapped on the wrong side, either, but Buster, racing ahead, had stopped to look back at me and I wanted to know what was around the next bend, so I stepped up the pace. Maybe unconsciously I knew that that house we'd seen from the tower had to be fairly near, and maybe we could get a better view of it beyond that hulking rock.

Dad and Crystal had fallen behind; the boys were on ahead now, with Buster frolicking between them and chasing driftwood sticks they threw. I was by myself when I rounded the end of the rock obstruction and looked up.

And there it was. Not like our house, set back a bit from the edge of the cliff, but right out on the edge. Three stories high, plus the tower above that. It was painted a soft green, with accents on the elaborate gingerbread in a darker green. It looked a lot like the Carson mansion that had been pictured on the front of the brochure outlining the historic tours.

They had a stairway descending to the beach, too,

zigzagging across the face of the cliff. And not too far ahead of us I spotted the indentation in the shoreline that was protected somewhat from the open sea by another jutting rock that curved toward us, making a sort of semi-bay.

I glanced around to see if Dad and Crystal were following. They weren't. They had found a huge log washed up at the base of the cliff and had sat down to rest. When Dad saw me looking, he waved a beckoning arm. I couldn't hear what he yelled, but I waved and ran forward to stop the boys from going any farther.

"Hey, look, Nikki, this is shallower and warmer," Sam cried as soon as I was close enough. "The waves don't even come in all the way here, not hard enough to knock you down the way they did below our place. I'll bet we could swim here."

I lifted my eyes to the house far above. "It may be a private beach," I said. "People live almost straight up from here."

"Hey, that's a neat house," Jeremy said. "Can we go up and look at it closer?"

"I don't think so. It would be rude. Dad's waving us to turn around and not go any farther."

"So soon?" Sam gave me a disgusted look. "Criminy. We just got here. Come see how much warmer the water is here."

The surf didn't seem to be climbing up the beach too rapidly, so I joined them in the shallower water. It was warmer; it felt delicious on my half-frozen feet.

The sand was warm, too, when we turned around and stayed out of the surf. The boys were running, wrestling, jumping all around, and Buster tried to keep up with them. I hoped they wouldn't give him a heart attack; he was pretty old for a big dog, though right now he was acting as if he were a puppy.

From where Dad and Crystal were waiting, you couldn't see the green house. The boys were urging them to come see the little semi-bay, and feel the warmer water, but Crystal shook her head. "This is far enough for me. And I don't think you'd better play anywhere on the beach without supervision."

"Can Nikki supervise?" Sam demanded immediately. "She's old enough."

"We'll see," Dad told him, getting up off the log. "If you don't think the tide comes in here with a lot of force, take a look at this monster log it washed all the way to the bottom of the cliff. That took some power. One thing's understood right now, okay? No coming down to the beach without prior permission, and not without someone along to take responsibility for seeing you're safe. And that means that no matter which of us tells you to come home or get out of the water, you obey immediately without question. Whether it's Nikki or Crystal or me. You got that?"

They had it. The ocean was terrific. It was also dangerous. They had the rules, and the consequences of not following them, while not spelled out in detail, would be substantial.

We stayed on our own beach for a while longer, searching for treasures. Every time the tide came in, it brought something new to deposit on the sand. I loaded my jeans pockets with shells and carried the glass float. Maybe someday I'd have some friends coming around again, and have these to show them.

I left my window open that night so I could hear the surf as I went to sleep. Buster seemed quite happy to accompany me upstairs to sleep, and though I settled him on the rug beside the bed, I woke later in the night to find him snuggled heavily against my back.

I smiled, reached out to pat him, and went back to sleep, feeling safe and secure with him there. He wasn't Bonnie, but at least I could talk to him without feeling like an idiot.

Dad picked up a little folder that told when the high and low tides were, and he even bought us each a watch—including Jeremy—so we could keep track of the time. We wouldn't have any excuse for failing to return to our own stretch of beach before the tide came in and cut us off.

"If we *did* get trapped on the other side of that rock," Sam pointed out, "we could always go up that other set of stairs to that green house, couldn't we?"

Dad gave him a steely eye. "You will *not* get caught on the other side of the rock," he told him firmly.

"Yes, sir," Sam acknowledged at once. But I caught the glance the boys exchanged after Dad turned away, and resolved that anytime I was responsible for them, I'd keep very close track of them. Ten-year-old boys are not necessarily trustworthy against all temptations.

We had a good time while Dad was there. He was willing to spend hours with a book or just sunbathing while the boys and I combed the sand for treasures or waded in the edge of the surf. We never saw anybody on the beach except far down to the south, where a few others sometimes showed up.

On the occasions when we went up-shore and around the black rock, we never saw anyone on that beach, either, and I often looked up at the house, hoping to catch a glimpse of the inhabitants. I don't know why I was so fascinated with that house, except that it was a marvelous example of Victorian gingerbread trim and it had a tower. From there, anybody could see us, I was sure, and I kept expecting someone to run us off, but they didn't. I never saw a soul, and a couple of times we played around in the shallow, warmer water below them, when Dad wasn't with us to object.

Crystal never went with us when Dad planned any kind of an outing. She always said she had to work. And finally she brought down a stack of the pen-and-ink sketches she'd been working on, for us to inspect. I don't think she wanted to, but Sam kept asking, and Dad encouraged her to share them with us.

I wasn't prepared for Crystal's drawings.

Oh, I knew she had to have some skills, to be a professional, or she wouldn't be illustrating books for B&B.

But these, simple as they might be, of small plants and ferns, were exquisite.

She heard me suck in my breath involuntarily as I approached the dining room table where she'd spread them out, and looked quickly at me.

I don't know what she'd expected. Maybe that I'd sneer at them, or turn away in disinterest.

"These are beautiful," I said, and beside me the boys concurred appreciatively.

"Wow!" Sam exclaimed. "I'll bet you're good enough to work for Disney."

Crystal relaxed enough to laugh, then. "Probably not," she said.

She hadn't wasted a pen stroke. There were feathery ferns, some still delicately furled, others intricately sketched in minute detail. The petals of a flower, even in black and white, were real enough to make you want to pick them.

"Can you draw me?" Jeremy asked eagerly.

She looked at him seriously. "I'm not as good with faces as I am with inanimate objects."

"Jer's an inanimate object," Sam offered, and they both giggled. But Jeremy asked again. "Can you, Mrs. Simons?"

She continued to stare at him. "I never do my best work unless I'm being paid," she teased, in a way we had not yet seen in her.

Jeremy promptly pulled out a quarter and slapped it on the table. "That's all I have on me."

Solemnly, Crystal picked up the quarter, then reached for the sketchbook she carried around much of the time. "Okay. Sit down there and hold still," she told him.

Ten minutes later, she handed over the page. I moved around to see it, too, and saw Jeremy's delight reflected clearly on his face.

"Wow!" Sam said, for the likeness, though without the detail of her book illustrations, was uncanny. Jeremy's pug nose, his freckles, his spiky hair, had been rendered unerringly.

"Now me," Sam clamored. "Do me next!"

She did Sam, and then me, after a questioning glance. I wouldn't have been brave enough to demand, the way the boys had, but I didn't actually want to be left out, either.

Dad came in from doing something with the van and stood looking at the finished portraits. "See, I told you she was good, didn't I?"

"Do Dad, too," Sam begged, but Crystal suddenly turned shy again.

"It will take longer to do him," she demurred. "I'll do him later, when I have more time." She spoke then directly to Dad. "I only have two more to do, and then I'm finished with this job. Are we going to mail them, or will you take them to Seattle yourself?"

"I'd feel safer hand-delivering them. Maybe the first of the week?"

Crystal nodded, and began restacking the sketches she'd brought down for us to see. I couldn't help thinking how much Mom would have appreciated them. But of course if Mom were still alive, we would never even have met Crystal.

Later that afternoon, Dad and I went into Trinidad for some bread and milk and stuff like that at the general store. He always asked Crystal if she wanted to go pick out things herself, but she never did. I wondered if she'd still be like this once she got her illustrations finished.

The store only had a couple of customers. A boy a little older than I was, sweeping the floor, paused to look up as we entered.

"Hi. Can I help you find anything?"

"More than likely," Dad said, producing his list and handing it over.

The boy set aside his broom, and I studied him as he read the list.

Tallish, with fair hair and tanned skin, he was wiry and muscular. He was wearing jeans and a nondescript T-shirt, with worn athletic shoes. He was, I decided, kind of cute.

"Milk. In the case, over there. Bread's at the far end, there. Matches, got some right here. Canned soup— what kind you want?"

A trio of boys about the same age came through the front door, and one of them called out, "Hey, Spook! You get in any of those peanut bars I asked about?"

"They should be in tomorrow," the boy helping us told them. "You want to pick out your soup here, sir?" he said to Dad.

While we were doing that, the newcomers continued to rag at the boy they'd called Spook. It was an unusual nickname, and I couldn't help wondering why they called him that. As he rang up our groceries, I suspected that he didn't appreciate it, though he kept his responses civil and to a minimum.

"Oh," I said, just as the boy announced our total, "Crystal mentioned needing Band-Aids. Do you have any?"

He told me where they were, and I went to get them. The door opened as I returned to the checkout stand, and a man in a wheelchair rolled in. He had a handful of mail, and was staring angrily at a letter he'd just opened.

The three boys who'd been trying to get a rise out of our clerk hastily moved past him and out the door. I got the distinct impression that they'd left in a hurry because of the man in the chair.

"Look at this!" he said, and slammed down the letter on the counter so the boy could see it. "She's not coming! What am I supposed to do now?"

The boy they'd called Spook smoothed out the sheet of paper and looked down at it. "Maybe you can find someone else to come and do it."

"Where? Where am I supposed to find a computer expert who'll stay in the house? And I've already tried among the locals. They don't want to come even in the daytime."

He was about Dad's age, I thought, maybe early

to middle forties. He had fair hair, what there was of it, and he was clean-shaven. He'd have been rather attractive if he hadn't been so furious.

Spook, for lack of a better identification, glanced at us apologetically. "Sorry. My father's just learned that the lady he hired to come and type up his manuscript on the computer he just bought isn't going to come, after all."

I spoke without thinking. "There are lots of people who can use a computer."

"Not around here, there aren't," the man almost snarled. "Not who are willing to work." He gave me a quelling look. "I suppose you're one of the experts, are you?"

Taken aback, I wished I'd kept my mouth shut. "Not exactly. But I'm used to sending E-mail, and doing school reports and things on the computer."

Dad had been distracted by the contents of a big freezer and hadn't overheard all of this. He'd certainly have noticed a reference to typing up a manuscript if he'd heard a mention of it.

"Can you type something onto a computer from a handwritten notebook?"

"I guess so. If I could read the handwriting," I remembered to add. I'd have hated to transcribe something my dad had written. His handwriting was atrocious.

So quickly that I jumped back out of the way, he grabbed for his offending letter and scrawled something on it, then thrust it at me. "Can you read that?"

I held it in place as Dad approached carrying a handful of ice-cream bars. "Can I add these? Sorry, am I interrupting something?"

I didn't answer, instead reading aloud what the man had written. "'This is a confounded nuisance.'"

"Dad," Spook said, placatingly, "this isn't the time or the place—"

"Then where is the time or the place? Blast it, this young lady says anybody can type something onto a computer. I can't, and you won't, and she can read my handwriting, miserable though it is. Do you want a job, young woman? I assume you're out of school for the summer."

I felt my jaw sagging. Several curious customers were waiting around, listening. Dad was standing there, letting the frozen bars begin to melt in his hand until he remembered to put them on the counter with the rest of our stuff.

He smiled a little. "I think the gentleman just offered you a job, Nikki. Do you want it?"

7

Of course it wasn't that simple. Dad had to know who the guy was—Hudson Gyasi—and where he lived—he gave a Trinidad address—and have some verification of the man's credentials and veracity.

By this time, I was afraid Dad would blow my chances by asking so many questions. But my dad wasn't going to just assume that the man was a legitimate employer, safe for me to be around. I prayed Dad wouldn't ask him for a character reference that would make him so angry, he'd tell me to forget it.

About that time, a Humboldt County sheriff's deputy walked into the store for an espresso and a dough-nut and greeted Mr. Gyasi by name. A minute later, the manager of the market returned from an errand and did the same, glancing curiously at Dad and me.

"I wouldn't want my daughter typing anything improper," Dad stated, getting back to business. By this time, they'd had to stick the ice-cream bars back in the freezer temporarily while all this was being settled.

I thought Mr. Gyasi himself seemed annoyed at this inquisition, but Dad was even-temperedly persistent. "You understand, I'm sure, that I can't have my daughter working for anyone questionable. Or typing pornography, for instance."

The man in the wheelchair went red in the face but kept his voice under control. "You're at liberty to see the manuscript for yourself, sir, if you like. I assure you it is nothing in the least objectionable, except that she may find it boring. Young people are often bored by scholarly works." He cast a malevolent glance at his son, who was standing by.

"That would seem appropriate to me," Dad said. "To see what Nikki would be typing, and where she'd be working." I'm not sure that Mr. Gyasi found it satisfactory; I had the impression he wasn't used to be challenged on such grounds, but he stood by his offer to let Dad check it out.

I'd only imagined applying for my first job, and had had no idea what it might turn out to be, but I'd thought

I'd be asked questions, which I'd answer to the best of my ability, and that I would then be permitted to ask a few questions of my own. Such as, *What does it pay?*

I never got a word in edgewise.

"What is the pay scale for this work?" Dad asked.

"The same as I would have paid the professional computer operator who was scheduled to come until she so inconveniently broke her arm." His lack of compassion for the lady made me blink.

He scribbled on the letter that still lay on the counter, and handed it over to Dad. I caught a glimpse of it and had visions of being able to buy all my school clothes in the fall and maybe even a used computer of my own instead of having to borrow Dad's when it wasn't in use.

"And this work would be done at your residence, rather than in a regular office?"

Gyasi made an angry gesture with his right hand. "As you see, I am confined to this chair. I have only limited use of my left hand, which makes learning to use the keyboard virtually impossible. My office is in my home. I have a housekeeper, Mrs. Mallory, who would stand as a chaperon. She can be recommended by her priest."

I wondered if Mr. Gyasi was always this rather choleric shade of pink, or only when his statements were challenged.

I also wondered how difficult he'd be to work for,

though typing a manuscript from handwritten copy seemed like something that wouldn't require his constant supervision. And I was remembering the figures he'd written on the letter. If it turned out not to be as good an opportunity as I'd hoped, would Dad let me quit before the job was finished? The financial incentive made me tingle a little in anticipation.

"Maybe we could drive out to your house," Dad suggested, "so that I could meet your housekeeper? And see the general layout of where Nikki would be working."

Mr. Gyasi's swallow seemed another attempt to control his resentment of this scrutiny. "Of course," he said in a clipped tone. "Mrs. Mallory is waiting for me in the car. If you care to, you can follow me home now."

He swung the mechanized chair around in expert fashion, but the boy who was waiting on us called after him. "Dad? Did you come in to get something?"

The back of Mr. Gyasi's neck got redder. "I require some antacid tablets," he said, and headed out the door without waiting for his son to fetch them until after he'd rolled his chair up a low ramp into a waiting metallic bronze van.

Dad refrained from comment about the antacid tablets until we'd fastened our own seat belts and fallen in behind the other vehicle. "He seems to suffer from a sour stomach," Dad said. "Hard to tell if his disposition results from that or if it's just his natural temperament. You sure you want to consider this, Nikki?"

I wasn't sure, but I'd never earned a paycheck in my life for anything other than something simple like picking berries or delivering flyers on my bike. "Can I quit if he's horrid?"

Dad considered. "Well, I'd want you to make a sincere effort to do it, if you agreed to. And there will be plenty of less-than-perfect bosses ahead of you, no doubt. You might have to get used to some along the way."

"But if he's really, *really* nasty, can I quit, even if I haven't finished the job?"

"If he hits you or swears at you, certainly," Dad said.

I looked at him in dismay to see if he was kidding. He wasn't kidding. I thought he meant it.

I licked my lips. "If he thinks I'm stupid? Too slow?"

"You're not stupid, and you're an excellent key-boarder. You're faster than I am."

"Dad, everybody is faster than you are!" I protested, and then he did grin.

"Let's check out Mrs. Mallory and the house, and the computer, okay? Then we'll decide."

We followed the van with its handicapped license plate out of the village of Trinidad and turned north on the freeway. We passed our own turnoff, and as we reached the next one and followed the bronze van, a prickle of excitement ran up my spine.

"Dad, isn't this about where the road would go off to that Victorian house we can see from the tower?"

"Could be. Might be classy digs to work in, kiddo. Of course, there may be a dozen houses along this road besides the one out on the cliff."

There weren't. We saw one log cabin, back in the woods, and another larger, modern house closer to the road, and then the route snaked around huge trees until we finally emerged on a gravel drive.

And there it was.

Up close, we could see that the green paint was weathered, the same as our own, but it was still a gorgeous house. Three tall stories, with a tower rising high above that, perched on the very edge of the cliff. You couldn't even walk around the front of the house on the ground, only across a veranda that wrapped the main floor.

We met Mrs. Mallory when she pulled onto a paved area. She came toward us, smiling, as we got out of the car behind her.

She was an older woman, rather comfortably plump, with gray hair and blue eyes.

"Do you need to help your employer before you talk to us?" Dad asked.

She laughed. "Not that one! It's worth your life to offer," she told me, and I thought it was a warning. "If he wants you to do anything, he'll tell you. Don't ever assume that he's helpless, or refer to him as a cripple."

Sure enough, the ramp on the far side of the van had descended, and the motorized wheelchair was rolled out and across the blacktop to another ramp that quickly took the man up to the veranda level.

"Come in, come in," Mrs. Mallory invited them. "Mr. Gyasi tells me you want to be sure this is a safe place for your daughter to work at typing up his manuscript on that extraordinary machine. He'd have me doing it if I were forty years younger, but I'm too old to learn that folderol. I thought Julian might be forced into doing it—he knows about the computer, but he's more interested in music. Not like my grandson—we can't get him away from those computer games. When his father is too impatient, Julian resists." She smiled more broadly and, I thought, with affection. "He may be only fifteen, but he has a bit of a backbone, and he says typing is not his thing. He'd rather work down at the store or play that guitar, and I was glad to see that when he put his foot down, he made it stick."

Julian. I never knew a boy named Julian before. I was pleased to know his real name. Without thinking further, I blurted out, "Why do the kids call him Spook?"

Her smile vanished. "Horrid little brats, they are. Ah, come right in this way," she said, leading the way, without really answering my question.

We had come in through a side entrance hall, and I saw that inside, this house had been beautifully kept. The wooden floors and the balustrades on the stairs were polished to a gleaming finish, and the colored glass windows around and in the door itself cast multi-hued patterns across the surfaces.

Fourteen-foot ceilings, Dad had said, and I glanced up at them. At the landing on the stairs, another stained-glass window illuminated the upper part of the stairway.

There was a dining room on one side of the entry, where I caught a glimpse of a glittering crystal chandelier, and a room with closed double doors on the other side. There was no sign of Mr. Gyasi. Mrs. Mallory didn't hesitate, but led us toward the side of the house facing the sea, and into a room that had almost as spectacular a view as we'd had from our tower.

It was set up as an office. There was a long worktable, spread with neat stacks of papers and a few books, two walls of floor-to-ceiling bookcases, and an obviously new and modern desk with a computer.

"Can you really work that thing?" Mrs. Mallory asked.

I walked over and took a look at it. "I think so," I said, reaching out to push buttons to turn it on. A familiar screen appeared: Windows. "Yes, this is the same program we use," I told her.

"Oh, good. Mr. Gyasi would have been so upset if you couldn't make it work. And he said he showed you an example of his handwriting, and you could read that?" She waited worriedly for my affirmation. "Sometimes I have trouble with it," she confessed, and I hoped that the sample I'd seen was the same as the rest I'd be expected to interpret.

"He said to show you, sir, the manuscript she'll be transcribing. It's this pile here, in this box."

She moved it where we could see it. Dad got first look, naturally. "It's a history of Humboldt County and Eureka? Sounds as if it shouldn't be anything objectionable."

"Oh, no, sir! Mr. Gyasi wouldn't have anything the young lady couldn't read! It's very scholarly, I believe. And quite proper."

And probably boring, I thought. But if I got paid for copying whatever it was, what difference did that make? Dad had to wade through some pretty boring stuff sometimes, trying to find manuscripts worthy of publication by B&B. It was part of the job, he said, though of course if it was *too* boring, or badly written, he didn't read the entire manuscript. Once Bonnie asked how many he had to read to find one that was good enough, and he'd said matter-of-factly, "Oh, I can accept maybe one in a thousand." The odds for a beginning writer, if that's what Hudson Gyasi was, were not very good.

I wondered if Mr. Gyasi's book was good enough to be accepted by a standard publishing house, or if he was planning to self-publish. I read a little bit on one of the pages from the box, and decided that it was probably literate enough; the grammar and spelling looked okay. That didn't necessarily mean it wouldn't be boring.

"What do you think, Nikki?" Dad asked.

"I'd like to try it," I said, suppressing my nervousness.

"Okay. Mrs. Mallory, I don't want to insult you as I may have done with your employer, but he said I could get a character reference for you from your priest? I want to be sure I'm not letting Nikki get into anything that might cause problems."

"Oh, I understand perfectly, sir! I'll write his name down for you, and the phone number, if you want it. He's at Saint Bernard's, in Eureka. These days, you can't be too careful."

She selected a sheet from a pile of blank paper and wrote on it, handing it to him. "He said if you're willing to work, you can report tomorrow morning at eight," she added, turning to me.

Eight. I winced inwardly. No sleeping in during vacation. But there'd be a paycheck at the end of the week, or the month, or the job. I didn't have any idea how long it would take to transcribe that box full of handwritten pages. A week? A month, at least, maybe more.

"You'll bring me back, won't you, Dad?" Our houses weren't very far apart by the beach, but since each was at the end of a long secondary road or driveway in from the main road, walking around that way would be four or five miles.

"Sure. Or, if I'm not available, Crystal can run you over and pick you up," Dad agreed.

So I had a job. And I'd met an interesting boy, Julian Gyasi. I wondered if he'd be around the house any of the time that I was here, or if that was too much to hope for.

I tried not to dwell too long on Mr. Gyasi and his antacid tablets. Hopefully he'd just been having a bad morning and wasn't dyspeptic all the time. Hopefully, too, he'd leave me alone in this room to work and wouldn't be standing—well, sitting—over me the whole time.

As Mrs. Mallory let us out, I commented, "This is certainly a beautiful house. Do you know how old it is?

"Oh, yes, it was completed in eighteen ninety-six. The original owner was one of the lumber barons, when they were still allowed to cut down the redwoods. The whole place is built of redwood, you know. It doesn't rot and is impervious to insects. These old places will stand forever, they're so sturdy. It's even fire resistant, the redwood is, did you know that?"

I hadn't known that. I was speculating on how I could manage to see the rest of the house after I came here to work. It was clearly much more elegant and special than the house Crystal had inherited from her aunt. I practically itched to see into the other rooms. Would there be an opportunity to see it all? Especially with Julian as a guide?

Julian, I decided, could almost cancel out his father, if he were around instead of working at the store in Trinidad. That wasn't something I felt I could ask Mrs. Mallory, especially in front of Dad.

We went back to the store to pick up the ice-cream bars, and Dad decided to buy some steaks for dinner, and returned to our own place.

The boys were fixing a snack of peanut-butter-and-banana sandwiches and chocolate milk. Jeremy grinned at me. "I tried some of that juice in the refrigerator. I thought it was orange juice. But it was carrot! Yuk!" He made a face.

"It's not bad," Dad told him, "especially with apple juice in it." He was making his own yuk face over their choice of sandwich filling. "Did you guys eat the last of the salami, or can a poor old starving father get a decent lunch?"

Crystal, we were informed, had already eaten without us. Dad decided to take his lunch up and join her, when the cell phone he had clipped to his pocket rang.

"Simons here," he answered it, juggling his plate in the other hand. Then he uttered a mild curse word, something he seldom did, and lowered the paper plate onto the table. "How bad is it?"

We all knew to stop talking and wait. Crystal, coming down the stairs right then, also picked up on the signal and came to a halt. "Something wrong?" she mouthed at me, and I hunched my shoulders to signify I didn't know yet.

"Okay," Dad said into the receiver. "Okay, I'll be there as soon as I can."

Concerned for family first, Crystal asked, "Bonnie?"

My heart lurched, but before that horrible possibility—bus wreck? hurricane? some tropical disease?—could completely form, Dad was hanging up and shaking his head.

"Not Bonnie. Old Mr. Billock's had a heart attack. He's in Harborview." That's Seattle's major trauma center. "They want me back there five minutes ago."

"I'll start throwing things together to leave immediately," Crystal said quickly.

"No, no sweetie, I can't wait for all of you and drive home. I'll have to fly. Nikki, get me the phone book, will you? I'll see when I can get a plane out of Eureka. If I'm lucky, I may not have to be gone more than a day or two."

Crystal had been concerned. Now she looked panicky. "Jeff—"

I brought the phone directory and he was already flipping through the yellow pages. "I have to go, sweetheart. Junior's falling apart." Junior was Mr. Billock's son, his second in command after Mr. Brandbury. "Nobody knows how bad it is yet, but chances are I can come back soon, maybe day after tomorrow. Hello? I need to book a flight to Seattle as soon as possible. Yes? Okay, hold me a seat on it. Jeff Simons." He rattled off his cellphone number and dug out a credit card to add to it. "You'll have to drive me to the airport, Crystal. They have a plane taking off in less than an hour. It's only a few miles. The kids should be okay here by themselves for that long, won't you, guys?"

And so we didn't get to tell Crystal about the new job until after Dad was gone and we were on our own.

And that was when everything seemed to start falling apart, without Dad there to fix it.

8

Dad made his flight at the last minute. Crystal came home and started checking to see what we could have for supper.

"There's no point in broiling those good steaks for just us," she said, and for a moment she sounded like Mom. "I'll stick them in the freezer and save them until your father comes back. We'll have something like toasted cheese sandwiches." Only when she looked in the refrigerator, her face fell. "Somebody ate all the cheese."

"I saw some cheese blocks—this good, aged cheddar that Dad likes so much—at the store in Trinidad," I said. "Let's run in and get some."

That was the first time she looked nervous. Over what? A two-mile drive to a town with hardly any traffic?

"Maybe we've got enough canned chili for one meal," she said.

Jeremy spoke up. "I'm allergic to the tomatoes in chili."

"Corned beef hash?" She was checking Aunt Edna's pantry. "No, there's only one can. That won't go around for four people."

"Let's go to the store," Sam urged. "Get some cheese for sandwiches, and some more of those ice-cream bars. Dad should have bought more in the first place instead of only enough for lunch."

Crystal looked as if we'd cornered her, like a wild animal. "I was trying not to have to go to the store until your dad comes back."

"But he may be gone a couple of days," Sam pointed out. "We've already eaten most of the fresh stuff we brought with us. Come on, Crystal, drive us into town."

The boys didn't notice anything out of the ordinary, but it was clear to me she didn't want to go. "I wish I could drive, but I can't," I said. "Sam's right. Let's go into Trinidad. It would be smart to get enough to last for several days, anyway. Don't we need milk, too, and more carrots if you're going to juice them?"

She wavered a few more minutes. "Well, all right,"

she finally conceded. "Let me change my clothes. I don't want to go to town in these."

She'd gone to the airport in them. What was the difference?

"If you don't want to get out of the car, I'll go in and get the stuff," I offered. "So you won't have to change."

She went to change, anyway. Out of jeans and a knit shirt into slacks and a long-sleeved blouse. And a hat. I hadn't even known she owned a hat. We've never seen her wear one before. It was broad-brimmed and she tied it on with a ribbon under her chin. She could hardly see out from under it.

"All right," she said when she came back to the kitchen. "Nikki can go in. Here's the list and the money."

Only Crystal stayed in the car, and she'd parked at the far end of the lot, where there weren't presently any other cars. Almost, it occurred to me, as if she were hiding inside the car and under the hat. But what sense did that make?

The boys wanted a whole bunch of stuff besides what was on the list. "No, no candy bars, you know how Dad feels about those," I said. "No gum. How about popcorn? We could pop corn."

While we were getting our stuff together, the same three boys I'd seen earlier came in. Immediately they began hassling Julian Gyasi. "Hey, Spook! How much for the watermelon?"

He told them in an even tone, not looking at them. Actually, the price was posted right on the bin.

Sam stared at the boy who had spoken. His black T-shirt had a slogan written across it in bright red. SUPPORT SEARCH & RESCUE. GET LOST. "Why do you call him Spook?" Sam asked.

The boy seemed to waver between ignoring a younger kid and wanting to further annoy Julian. "Because he lives in a haunted house. Spook from a haunted house. Get it?"

I stiffened. Haunted house? That beautiful mansion on the cliff was haunted?

Not that I believed in ghosts, naturally. But I resented the way the kid was treating a boy who wasn't doing anything to *him*. "Do you have any more of that deli potato salad?"

Julian looked right at me. "Sorry. We'll have some more tomorrow. The macaroni's pretty good. You want a taste of it?"

"Sure," I said, and accepted a plastic spoonful. "Um, yes. Give me one of the big containers of that."

The second of the trio of boys decided to get into the act. He was tall and skinny and wore a cap with

KENNY on it. "We heard some tourist girl was going to work up at the spook house, using the computer. You the one?" he asked me.

"I'm going to be transcribing a manuscript for Mr. Gyasi," I said, suddenly tense.

The shorter, plumper one who kept referring to Julian as Spook laughed and stepped closer to me. "You're braver than I am, lady."

I hoped the tremor that ran through me wasn't visible. "Right," I said, smiling. "I probably am."

He didn't like that, but I thought Julian did. His mouth quirked ever so slightly. "Will there be anything else?" he asked quietly.

"I think the boys found some more chips," I said, adding them to the stack on the counter, turning my back on the local boys who weren't anybody I wanted to get better acquainted with.

"She's smarter, too," my little brother contributed. Obviously it hadn't occurred to him that we were outnumbered and outweighed. But nobody jumped us.

Even Julian's tormentors were laughing now—two of them, anyway. "She's got you there, Arnie," the third boy said.

Julian had totaled our order, and I handed over the cash. When we turned to leave, the mouthy Arnie was standing so close to me, I almost walked into him. He glared at me in a menacing way that might have made me quite uneasy if it hadn't been for the uniformed deputy who walked in right then.

The officer called out to Julian, "My usual, please," and then spoke to the other boys. "You kids better move your bikes. Somebody's going to trip over them."

With muttered responses, they moved off without speaking any further to us.

The cop seemed to sense the tension in the store. "They bothering you?" he asked Julian.

"They were rude to her," he said, tipping his head in my direction.

"Really? They give you any trouble, young lady, you let me know. They may have forgotten that we can find things for rude people to do other than harass visitors." He smiled, and he was very good looking, especially in uniform. He accepted his plastic cup of coffee and left.

"Did he make them do something before?" Sam wanted to know. "For being rude?"

Julian grinned every so slightly. "Not *speaking* rude. They wrote obscenities with paint on the pavement in the parking lot. He made them spend an afternoon on their knees with wire brushes and solvents, getting it all off."

"Cool!" Sam approved, and Jeremy echoed him.

We carried our bags back to the car. Crystal swung around to stare at us as we loaded them in the van. "What was that all about?"

"Some smart-aleck kids mouthed off," I said, "and the cop made them move their bikes. That's all." I don't know why I didn't want to tell her the whole thing, except that she was already so nervous about something, it didn't seem sensible to make it worse.

The boys had to tell her about scouring off the obscenities in the parking lot. She seemed to relax a fraction, not terribly interested in adolescent boys who had been stupid and got caught. As soon as we were all belted in, she started the engine and we went straight home without further incident.

I had lots of questions, though. The boys had been unpleasant, not just to Julian but to us. I decided I'd better warn Sam not to provoke them if we encountered them again. There might not be a sheriff's deputy on hand next time.

And I was dying of curiosity about the supposedly haunted house. Were they just being hateful to say I must be brave to go to work for Mr. Gyasi? There couldn't really be anything dangerous about working up there, could there?

Of course not. The boy named Arnie had been being spiteful, trying to get a rise out of Julian.

Usually it was Dad who went around locking doors at night, making sure the house was secure. He said when he was a kid, nobody worried about whether a door was locked or not, but you had to be more careful these days.

So I wasn't surprised when Crystal checked all the doors. I was a little taken aback when she tested all the windows as well, making sure none of them had been left unlocked. She even closed and slid the bar on the door between the kitchen and the pantry/utility room. When she saw me watching her, she grimaced. "It doesn't pay to take chances," she said.

I didn't make any comment. I had no problem with locked doors. All you had to do was watch the news on TV to hear about robberies and attacks on innocent citizens. I had no desire to be among them.

Buster had already gotten into the habit of following me up to bed. Sometimes he sneaked off to join the boys for a while, no doubt because they had snacks after they'd gone to bed. But as soon as he thought he'd found all the crumbs, he'd come trotting into my room. "On the rug, Buster," I'd tell him. And obediently he'd lie down there. But as soon as I went to sleep, he'd be up on my bed, curling against me. Nights were cool here, and I didn't object to the extra warmth. But it occurred to me, as I was drifting off, that having someone to snuggle up to might be part of what Dad meant about wanting to be married again. Not that Crystal was like a dog, but she must be warm and comforting on a chilly night.

Later, I woke up in complete darkness, startled without knowing why. There were no streetlights, no yard light, here. Only velvety blackness, pressing in around me. Buster was a heavy lump against my legs, but the room had gotten fairly cold.

I lay still, heart unaccountably thumping. Why?

And then I heard it, what must have aroused me in the first place.

A protesting moan, rising in intensity, somewhere in this house. And as it rose into a near-scream, I felt the hair lifting off the top of my head in blind horror.

9

That ungodly moan brought me upright, immediately aware that Dad was not in the house.

The sound dwindled into a sort of choking gurgle. I moved to swing my legs over the edge of the bed, eliciting a grunt from Buster when I shifted position, though he didn't wake up. Some watchdog he was. Maybe Dad was right, that he was getting a bit deaf in his old age.

I jabbed him with an elbow, and he grunted again, then raised his head against my outstretched hand.

"Get up, Buster! You're coming with me," I said, knowing I couldn't just burrow under the covers and wait for whatever was going to come next.

I reached for the lamp, remembered it was on the

opposite side of the bed from the one at home, and flopped over to turn it on.

It was a small bulb—nobody'd ever be able to read in bed in this room—but it sent a welcome circle of light around me. My traveling digital clock showed 12:07 A.M.

Buster was looking at me as if I'd lost my mind. Then, when the sounds were repeated, he lifted his ears and jumped off the bed to follow me.

The door to the boys' room stood open, and I hesitated there. Nothing from them. I knew Dad had brought a flashlight, but I thought he'd kept it in the master bedroom, so I didn't have it.

I crept along the chilly hallway in my bare feet, and the moan was repeated, this time with words: "No! No!"

I hesitated at the door of the room where Crystal was sleeping alone. The light from my open doorway didn't come this far, certainly not into the room.

"Crystal?" I asked hesitantly, praying she wasn't being strangled in her bed by some fiend who had gotten in in spite of locked doors and windows.

For a moment there was no sound, and then she gasped and I sensed movement.

"Crystal?" I said more loudly. "Are you all right?"

"Wha—? What is it?"

"What's wrong? Were you having a bad dream?"

"Dream," she muttered. "Nightmare, yes. Who is it—Nikki?"

"Yes. Are you okay?"

"Oh, it was . . . horrible. All that . . . blood. They were all dead. Just like . . ." Her voice trailed off. "Jeff, where's Jeff?"

"Dad had to go home to Seattle," I reminded her. The bare floor was icy beneath my feet and I was shivering.

"Oh. Oh, yes, I remember now." She inhaled raggedly. "I'm sorry. I'm awake now, Nikki. I'm sorry I woke you up."

"Do you have nightmares like this very often?" I asked uncertainly. It must have been a doozy, and I wasn't sure if I should leave her now or not. Dad would probably have put his arms around her in reassurance, but I didn't feel I could do that.

"Not so often anymore," she said. She was bringing her breathing under control. "It was so *real*. Oh, my heart is still racing. But it was all a dream, wasn't it?"

"Nothing else has happened," I told her. I remembered my own last nightmare, years ago, before Mom got sick. "Sometimes it takes awhile to get over it. Mama sometimes made me some cocoa and we talked until I calmed down."

"Cocoa. Yes, that would be good. Just a minute, let me find a robe. And slippers. Gosh, it's cold in here."

"I didn't bring a robe with me," I said, feeling colder by the minute.

Crystal emerged out of the darkness and thrust a garment into my hand. "Here, wear your dad's."

I shrugged into it, wrapping it tightly around me (it was almost big enough to wrap twice) and holding it in place by tying the belt. I still didn't have anything on my feet, but when we got downstairs there were some rag rugs and I slid one over in front of my chair at the kitchen table.

"I'm going to turn the furnace on for a little while," Crystal said, and pushed at the thermostat just inside the dining room door. "Where did we put the cocoa?"

I got it out while she brought milk and got down mugs. While she was heating milk in the microwave, I sat with my feet curled on the rug and thought about what she'd said when I woke her out of the nightmare.

It was horrible. All that blood. They were all dead. Just like . . . She hadn't finished that sentence. Just like . . . what? Had she really seen something like that at one time? People covered with blood? Dead? That would have given me nightmares, for sure.

And when I'd asked if she'd had them often, she'd said, *Not so often anymore.*

Meaning, I guessed, that in the past she'd had them

frequently. Always the same dream? About dead people, and blood?

Gradually the furnace heated the room, and I stopped shivering. When she brought the cups to the table, we stirred the cocoa to dissolve the powder and warmed our hands on the big china mugs before we drank.

She had been shaking when we reached the kitchen, turning on lights all the way. I didn't know if it was from the nighttime temperature of the house or from the nightmare, or both. She seemed to be calming down now, taking sips of the hot cocoa.

"It's good, isn't it? I'm glad you thought of it, Nikki."

"Are you all right now?" I asked.

"Just give me a little more time, and I will be. I wish your father hadn't had to leave us here."

"Me, too," I agreed. "Does Dad know you have nightmares like this? Really bad ones?"

It was a moment or two before she responded. "No. No, I haven't had one since we've been married." Her smile was wan. "It's nice to wake up next to someone after a dream like that. Thank you for coming and waking me up. I hope I didn't scare you."

Half to death, I thought, but didn't say it. "It took me a minute to realize what I was hearing."

"Thank you," she said again, and drained her cup. "I hope I can go back to sleep now."

We stood up and put our cups, unwashed, in the sink. I hesitated. Crystal had never demonstrated any particular fondness for animals, but I then asked, "Would you like to take Buster into your room for the rest of the night? I know he's not supposed to sleep on the beds, but he's really a clean dog, and he's nice and warm to curl up with, even when he's on the top of the quilts. I know you got pretty chilled."

That sounded better than mentioning her terror again, and pointing out that the presence of a big dog could be rather comforting.

Crystal hesitated, then nodded. "Thank you, Nikki. If he'll come with me, I'd like to have him."

Buster would go with any member of the family who invited him. I didn't know if he got onto the bed with her or not, which I would have invited him to do. I went back to bed myself, still wearing Dad's robe with the scent of his shaving lotion on it, and waited to get warm enough to go back to sleep, still pondering Crystal's words and knowing I wasn't brave enough to ask her to explain them further.

Maybe, I thought just before I fell asleep, I'd tell Dad about the nightmare and the things she'd said. Maybe he could figure it out. He certainly wouldn't be afraid to ask her.

The next morning was Sunday. We decided we were

smart enough to make pancakes—measure out the pancake flour and add water and fry them on the big griddle we'd found in the cupboard—so we were having a substantial breakfast.

"Are we going to church?" I asked. At home, we never missed a Sunday unless somebody was sick.

Crystal was taken aback. "I hadn't planned on it," she demurred immediately. "We don't know anybody here."

"We know God," Sam said unexpectedly. "He's everywhere the same, isn't he?"

"I don't even know where there's a church," Crystal said.

That struck me as absurd. There were churches all over the place. "There's at least one in Trinidad, only a few miles away. And Arcata and Eureka are full of churches. I saw the spires and the crosses when we were driving around."

"I . . . don't think I feel like going. I hadn't planned on it."

"What's to plan? This is tourist country. I doubt if anyone would object if we went in jeans, but we've all got something dressier than that. It would only take a few minutes to change."

"Not this week," Crystal said with more firmness than she usually displayed. "Maybe next week, when Jeff is back."

We could have gone by ourselves, but it was just a little too far to walk, I decided. The boys didn't really care. They voted for the beach.

"Oh," I said to Crystal as we were clearing the table, "I'll need a ride to my job tomorrow. Eight o'clock in the morning."

She nearly lost the sea of syrup still standing on Jeremy's plate, tilting it toward the sink just in time. "Job? What job?"

"I'm going to be transcribing a handwritten manuscript for the father of the boy who works at the general store. On a computer."

She stared at me as if I'd suddenly become a kumquat. "When did all this come about?"

"The day Dad left. He said it was okay, I'll earn enough money for my school clothes next fall, and maybe somewhere near enough to get me a used computer so I don't have to use Dad's."

"But you can't even know this person!"

"Does anybody usually know the people they go to work for? He's just a man in a wheelchair who can't use the computer himself, and he's written this book in longhand. You know you can't submit it that way—"

Crystal ran an agitated hand through her silvery hair, leaving it standing in wisps. I knew she had her moments of being beyond understanding, but I wasn't prepared for her vehemence. "No, I can't let you do this, Nikki."

Stupefied, I felt my jaw drop. "What do you mean you can't *let* me? Dad already said I *could.*"

"Your father isn't here," she snapped, as if the tension had suddenly become too much for her, though why it should have left me baffled.

"I know that. But he said I could. He talked to the man, and we went to his house and met his housekeeper, and Dad said I could do it. I'm expected to be there at eight in the morning, and I need a ride because it's too far to walk."

"No," Crystal said flatly.

Well, we'd not become bosom buddies, and I wasn't happy that my dad had married her, and I didn't expect we'd ever be best friends, but I certainly hadn't anticipated anything like this.

"I want to call Dad and ask him, then," I said finally. "He said I *could,* so I don't see how you can say I *can't.*"

"Because I'm in charge while he's gone," Crystal said, still in that flat, noncompromising tone.

"I'm calling Dad," I repeated. But when I tried, I couldn't reach him. He wasn't at home, and when I tried his office at B&B, he wasn't there, either. I even tried Harborview, thinking he might be at the hospital where

Mr. Billock was, but though they admitted Mr. B was a patient, they said there was no one visiting him at the moment and when they paged Dad, nobody answered. Surely he'd keep his cell phone on him, but he didn't answer that number, either. Frustration was at a boiling point.

It didn't make for a pleasant day. I smoldered, and Crystal went into her studio to work. We each fixed our own lunch—at different times—and didn't speak to one another all afternoon. I decided if she was in charge, she could deal with supper on her own, and I didn't even show up to clean vegetables for a salad.

Finally Sam pecked his head into my room and asked, "What's going on? How come nobody's fixing anything to eat?"

"Crystal informed me she's the boss while Dad's gone, and that I can't go to my new job, so we're not speaking," I told him. "Fix whatever you can find in the refrigerator. Eating junk for one night isn't going to hurt you any. By tomorrow, I'll be able to talk to Dad."

He regarded me with troubled eyes. "What are you going to do?"

"I told Mr. Gyasi I'd be there at eight, and I will be."

"You're going to walk all that way?"

I'd had time to think about it by this time. "It's too

far by road, but I can cut three or four miles off the distance if I go by the beach. Incidentally, unless *she* goes with you, you stay off the beach while I'm gone."

His dismay struck at my conscience, but what could I do about it? Of course Dad had expected to be here to look after the boys, but he hadn't changed any of the rules before he left.

I relented a little. "I don't know how long I'll have to work, but if I start at eight, I'd think I'd be able to come home by four or so. I'll go down to the beach with you then."

He brightened a little. "Can we watch for you from the top of the stairs? And come down when we see you coming?"

"I guess so, but don't start watching until at least four o'clock," I told him.

If Crystal got anything to eat that evening, it was when the rest of us weren't in the kitchen. I tried again to reach Dad at home, and had to leave a message on the answering machine. I didn't explain it—I thought I'd better tell him my side of the story in person—and just said I needed to talk to him as soon as possible.

I hoped he'd call back before I went to bed. He didn't. So I had to make up my own mind what to do.

I decided to simply get up early and walk over to the Gyasis' by way of the beach and the stairs. I didn't leave a note. If I didn't show up the next day, I figured Crystal would be smart enough to come to the conclusion that I'd walked to work without her permission.

Did I deliberately neglect to tell her where I'd be working? I don't know. Maybe. She wasn't being receptive to anything I said, and I had no reason to think it would matter to her where I went and who my employer was. At least that's what I told myself when I set the alarm for six-thirty the next morning.

Buster was back in bed with me that night, and I didn't steer him toward Crystal's room. If she had any nightmares, she kept them quieter. If she wanted Buster's company, she'd have to ask for it, but she didn't.

I slept restlessly, waking before the alarm went off. I didn't want it to wake Crystal up. I wasn't sure what she'd do if she knew I was defying her and going to work against her direct forbidding of it. But I wasn't eager to find out.

Why was she taking such an attitude? What difference did it make to her whether I took a job or not? Especially when I'd explained to her that Dad had met the man and his housekeeper and was satisfied that I'd be perfectly safe and that the material I'd be typing was acceptable?

I didn't put on my shoes until I got down to the kitchen. It was only a quarter of seven and Crystal wasn't likely to be up for some time yet. I ate cold cereal and a banana, and then, because nobody had said what I'd do about lunch, I made a sandwich and stuck an apple in a paper bag to take with me. I could always go down and eat on the beach if I needed to.

I'd allowed plenty of time to get over to the Gyasi house, but by the time I'd gone down our stairs, walked along the beach and around the jutting rock barricade separating our section from theirs, and up the other flight of stairs, I was winded.

Mrs. Mallory let me in, smiling. "Good morning, Nikki. Mr. Gyasi is waiting for you in his study."

"Am I late?" I asked in alarm, but she shook her head. "No, no, you're early. He's always up with the birds, often has trouble sleeping, poor man. He hurts quite a bit, you know."

"What happened to him?" I blurted, and then realized that maybe I'd better learn to curb my tongue.

"Oh, he was in a terrible accident. He never wanted to go back to teaching at the university after he was in that car wreck, though being in a wheelchair wouldn't have kept him from conducting classes. His wife died in the mishap, and that took the heart right out of him, they say. I didn't work for him then, only after he came back to Trinidad to live."

"I thought he'd always lived here," I said, trying to remember the conversation with Mr. Gyasi.

"Oh, he grew up in this house. It's belonged to his family practically forever." She led me along the hallway toward the study that overlooked the ocean. "But he went away to school and taught in a college somewhere. I forget which one, one of those prestigious ones. He only came home after the accident. He'd always owned the house, after his parents died, but he hadn't wanted to live here. But I suppose it seemed a reasonable place to bring his motherless son to grow up." She had been pleasant, smiling, but now her face twisted. "If only those miserable young whelps in the village weren't so unmerciful with Julian. I don't think he's especially happy here, but he's going away to school next year. Here you are. She's here, Mr. Gyasi."

The man swiveled in the mechanized chair to face us. "Well, at least you're on time," he said gruffly. "I'll show you the manuscript—here—and the paper you're to use. This for my copy, that heavier bond for finished copies, of which I'll need two. They're to be put into these boxes. I'll be checking them over for accuracy before they're shipped out, of course."

The look he gave me suggested that he thought I might try to get away with covering up my errors.

"There's a spell-checker on the computer," I told him quietly, subduing my nervousness. "It should catch any mistakes."

I could tell by his reaction that though he might have heard of spell-checkers, he didn't really know how they worked.

Without a further invitation, I sat down and turned on the computer, giving it a chance to warm up and give me a blank page. I typed out a line, deliberately misspelling a couple of words. "See? If the spelling is wrong, it makes a wiggly red line under the word. And if you click on it with the right side of the mouse," I demonstrated, "it gives the correct spelling, and then when you click again, it makes the correction on the screen."

He clearly knew nothing about computers. I wondered what he had taught, that he'd remained so uninformed about a tool that was so universally in use. I had the impression that he was impressed but not about to admit it—not with my knowledge of it, but with the computer's ability to detect misspelled words.

"What shall I do if there's a word I can't interpret?" I asked, reaching for the first page of his handwritten text. "Shall I come ask you, or mark it to check on later?"

"Ask me," he said. "I do not want any mistakes in what you print out."

"All right." I hesitated. "Do you have a publisher for this, or are you printing it yourself?"

Somehow he managed to draw himself taller in his chair, indignation barely under control. "It will be published," he informed me, which didn't answer my question. Maybe I should have kept still, but I was used to having some facts to work with.

"Self-published?" I persisted. "Or do you have a contract with a publisher, or will you be looking for one when it's been printed out?"

"It will not be necessary for me to self-publish," he said, so I got the idea that he expected to find a publisher, and that he was insulted that I would assume it wasn't good enough to find a commercial publisher who would pay him for it, rather than having to pay to get it into print. I knew enough to know that most professional authors expect to be paid, rather than having to pay a subsidy publisher.

"I'm asking because my dad's an editor," I explained. "At Billock & Brandbury Books, out of Seattle. So I've seen a lot of manuscripts." And I remembered how many books he had to read to find one worth publishing, but I didn't tell him that.

His nostrils flared perceptibly. I didn't think he'd ever heard of B&B. It wasn't one of the big New York companies like Simon & Schuster or Doubleday, but it was a respectable publishing house.

"You may begin," he said. "I will be just across the hallway in my own room, reading and revising the last few chapters. If you need to consult with me, you may knock on the door over there."

He wheeled away, leaving me to start the job. I was glad he wasn't standing over me, watching, because I made a few boo-boos before I got everything set up to do manuscript form pages, with numbers and margins set appropriately.

When I'd done the first chapter, I decided I'd better show it to him to make sure it was satisfactory before I went on. When I stood up, I could see the tranquil blue of the ocean beyond the big windows, with a freighter heading toward Humboldt Bay. I hoped the boys wouldn't go down on the beach without Crystal, and I wasn't sure how much time she'd be willing to spend with them, instead of in her studio.

I took in a deep breath and prepared to knock on the door of Mr. Gyasi's room and show him what I'd done so far. Actually, I thought it looked great. I knew the right format for printing it out, and he had a superb printer that turned out completely professional-looking material.

I opened the door into the hallway and ran right into a tall, bulky figure I hadn't been expecting. I gulped aloud and almost fell over backward, while this stranger's face stared down at me in what I could only describe as an unfriendly manner.

10

The man grunted and pulled away from me.

He was about fifty, I thought, with overlong graying hair and rather blank light-colored eyes. In the dimness of the hallway it was impossible to say whether they were gray, blue, or green. He wore bib overalls and a blue work shirt, and smelled of freshly cut grass.

"Sorry," I apologized, regaining my balance. "I was just taking these over to Mr. Gyasi—"

"Excuse me," he said, and I saw that he was twisting a baseball cap in his big hands. He reached out and rapped on the door of my employer's room.

"Come in," Mr. Gyasi called, and the man twisted the knob and went in, leaving the door open for me to follow.

"Yes, Bruce, what's the matter now?" The wheelchair swung around to face us, and the occupant frowned, whether at Bruce or at me I couldn't tell.

"I'm out of gas," Bruce said. "Can't mow anymore."

"Then go on and trim the hedge. I'll have Julian refuel the mower when he comes down. Yes, Nikki, what is it?"

"I thought you'd want to see how I did the first chapter before I went on to the second one," I said, moving forward as the man called Bruce put his hat back on and left.

He took the sheaf of papers and looked through them. "Hmm. Hmm. They look excellent," he said, and I felt my stomach muscles relax somewhat. "Nikki— what kind of name is that for a girl?"

"It's short for Nicole," I told him, wondering what my name had to do with anything.

"I shall call you Nicole," he announced. "Nikki sounds like a dog. Yes, this format will do nicely. You may do the finished copies on the heavier bond just like this."

"Thank you," I said, and scuttled backward out of the room, feeling as if I were leaving royalty upon whom I could not turn my back.

I was moderately stunned by his assertion that Nikki sounded like a dog. Oh, well, as long as he wrote something on my paycheck that made it possible to cash it, what difference did it make?

I was crossing the hallway when I heard someone coming down the stairs, and turned my head in that direction.

Julian Gyasi saw me and came toward me. "Hi. You got started, I see."

"Yes. And my first attempt passed muster." I held up the pages so he could see them. "I don't think there's going to be anything hard about it."

He glanced at his father's closed door. "Don't tell him that, or he won't want to pay you the full amount he agreed to."

I didn't say anything, but Julian grinned. "He's not stingy, really, but he is thrifty. Being without regular paychecks for a few years does that to you. If he sells this book, maybe he'll loosen up a little. Is it any good?" He hesitated. "The little bit I looked at was pretty stuffy."

I considered. "It's too early to tell, I think. Maybe the first part is a bit—dry—but history texts often are, aren't they? I think the stuff I noticed about the lumbering days, the logging of the redwoods, may turn out to be interesting."

"I hope so. If everybody turns it down, it won't improve his disposition. I'm just about to have breakfast. Can you take a break and join me?"

"I ate before I came," I told him, glancing at the closed door behind me. "And I don't know if I'm allowed breaks."

"Everybody's allowed breaks. I think it's a state law. Come on, you can have a drink of juice or coffee or something."

So I left the typed pages in the workroom and followed Julian into the kitchen. Like our house, it was old-fashioned, but I noticed they'd put in a dishwasher and a more modern-looking range.

The hired man, gardener, whatever Bruce was, was seated at the table, eating. He glanced at me, then quickly away.

Mrs. Mallory turned to us with a smile. "About time you came down, boy. You want ham and eggs this morning?"

"Sure. And toast and juice. Nikki here will have juice, at least. Or maybe one of those sticky buns I'm smelling?"

I agreed to that, and we sat at the opposite end of the table from Bruce, who looked up at Julian and then quickly away. "Out of gas," he said. "Hudson said you'd refill the mower."

"Okay," Julian responded. And then, to me he said, "I guess you're making out fine with the computer."

"It's the same program Dad has at home."

"Good. I'm glad someone other than me is willing to do it. How are you getting along with my dad?"

"I only saw him for a few minutes before I started, so it's okay so far," I told him. The sticky bun was still warm, yeasty, and full of butter and cinnamon and raisins, and I pulled off pieces of it. "Umm. This is very good. Better than my cold cereal was."

Julian nodded. "We're lucky to have a good cook. The trouble is, my dad has a funny stomach; he can't eat a lot of stuff, so she can't make it just for Bruce and me."

"Bruce is . . . the gardener?" I guessed, hoping the man wouldn't be insulted by that. I suspected he might be retarded, the way he kept ducking his head and avoiding a direct gaze. He had turned away then and was speaking to the housekeeper, something about the buns.

"Yeah. He's been here ever since we came back from Southern California two years ago." Julian lowered his voice. "He's not much of a conversationalist, but he keeps the grass cut and trims the hedges and weeds the flowers. Dad says we have to keep it nice looking in case we ever get enough money to move, so it'll be easier to sell."

"It's a beautiful place," I said around a mouthful of sticky bun.

"It belongs to Dad, so it doesn't cost us anything to live in it. I guess your family is renting the old Milan house for the summer?"

"Not renting, no. My stepmother inherited it," I said.

Instantly I was aware that Mrs. Mallory had paused in flipping eggs, and Bruce had swiveled around to face us again, though Julian didn't react to my statement. She waited until she brought his plate to the table before speaking with an air of casualness that didn't seem quite natural, though I couldn't have said why. "Your step-mother was related to Edna Milan?"

"Crystal was her niece," I said. "Did you know Mrs. Milan?"

"Oh, she wasn't *Mrs. Milan*. She was an old maid," Mrs. Mallory said. "I only knew her by sight. You know everybody that way in a town the size of Trinidad. You had enough buns, Bruce?"

The man grunted an affirmative, and drained his coffee cup. "Thanks," he said, and got up to leave.

They offered me another sticky bun, but I figured I'd better get back to work. "Is there a place I can wash my hands before I handle Mr. Gyasi's papers?"

Julian pushed back his chair, too. "I'll show you," he said, "and then I'll refuel the lawn mower before I go to work."

The powder room was tucked away in what I would have guessed to be a closet, under the stairs. "This must have been added as an afterthought," I said when Julian opened the door for me.

"Right. You ought to see the original bathrooms, upstairs. Big enough to be bedrooms, and impossible to warm up to a comfortable level," he said.

Before I could lose my nerve, I said, "I'd like to see the entire house sometime. Would that be possible?"

"Sure. I'll give you the guided tour the first chance I get. I don't go into work tomorrow until noon, so how about on your break tomorrow morning?"

"Do you work full-time at the store?" I asked, reluctant for him to go.

"No, part-time. I wouldn't mind working more hours, but I'm lucky to have a job this close to home so I can ride my bike. Did your dad bring you over today?"

"No, I walked along the beach." That stirring of resentment against Crystal for refusing to drive me around by the road wasn't something I could discuss with him, but I couldn't help still being angry with her.

"Yeah, it's too far to walk by the road. Well, see you later," Julian said, and left me.

I turned out a neat stack of beautifully printed pages. I even got a little bit interested in the text; the chapter on the words and terms used in the lumbering days was not as dry as some of the purely historical material. I even got caught reading ahead on some of it, not typing.

"Is there a problem with my writing?" Hudson Gyasi asked behind me. That wheelchair could move very silently, I thought, startled.

"No, I just . . . got interested in this part, and read

ahead," I admitted, hoping that the fact I hadn't been typing when he came in wouldn't count against me.

"Did you? I hope that will be the reaction of an editor who sees it," he commented. "Hmm. This looks quite acceptable. I hope Bruce didn't bother you."

"No. I wasn't expecting him in the hall, so I jumped when I opened the door and found him there. He never came in here."

"Nor should he. If he bothers you, speak to either Mrs. Mallory or to me. I assume you would like to take a break for lunch now. Mrs. Mallory informs me she has a pot of soup on, if you'd like to retire to the kitchen." When I hesitated, he added, "I will be eating in my room. I'm working on editing and also sorting pictures that will be used to illustrate the book."

"Are you using drawings? My stepmother does sketches to illustrate books," I told him.

I didn't get the impression that he was interested in what Crystal did. "No, these are photographs. Very old photographs." He made it sound as if they were quite superior to mere sketches, and perhaps they were.

I went through to the kitchen, where the aroma of homemade soup was more tantalizing than my dry sandwich. "Actually," I said, "I brought a sack lunch with me."

"Oh, heavens, no need to do that. I always have to fix

lunch for everyone else, and you might as well eat a hot meal," Mrs. Mallory said, so I sat and consumed two bowls of pea soup with generous chunks of ham in it, and homemade bread. Mr. Gyasi wasn't so stingy that he allowed her to ruin the bread; there was real butter to spread on it.

I was relieved that Bruce didn't come in for his lunch until I had nearly finished. For some reason he made me kind of uncomfortable, and I didn't know how to talk to him.

Mrs. Mallory wasn't talking to him, either, when I left, just putting a plate and a bowl in front of him.

The afternoon went by quickly, with more perfect pages stacking up. At least I thought they were perfect, until Mr. Gyasi came in and checked through them and handed one back. "There's a typographical error here," he pointed out.

My stomach lurched as I leaned over to see what he was indicating. "This word should be *so,* not *no.* It seems the wonderful machine does not catch all errors, after all," he said.

"Both are legitimate words," I pointed out. "If they're correctly spelled, the checker won't know which one it's supposed to be. I can fix that in a few seconds and replace that page."

I hoped he'd go away, but he stood there and watched

me do it. It was simple enough, and I didn't make any false moves, but I was nervous with him looking over my shoulder.

When the corrected page spurted out of the printer, he caught it, examined it, and nodded without speaking. He laid the finished pages in their box, and turned to leave, the wheels of his chair soundless on the polished wood floor.

I cleared my throat. "Um . . . we didn't discuss the time I would leave in the afternoon. Is four o'clock all right?"

"Four o'clock? Fine," he said, and left me alone to proceed to the next chapter

On the whole, it was a satisfying day. I hadn't made any major mistakes, not enough to get fired for.

I didn't exactly look forward to going home. I didn't know what Crystal was going to say. I'd have to try again to get hold of Dad and have him tell her that he'd given me permission to come this morning.

At precisely four, I shut down the computer and the printer and picked up the sack lunch I hadn't eaten at noon. I walked out through the silent house. Mr. Gyasi's door was closed and there was only silence behind it, and I didn't see Mrs. Mallory anywhere. I wondered what time Julian would be home from work. There was no sign of him so far.

I let myself out of the house and went down the ramp to the parking area, crossed it, and started down the long flight of stairs to the beach.

All of a sudden my back felt funny. As if someone was watching me.

I paused, hand on the railing, and looked around, but there was no one in sight. I even glanced up at the tower, far overhead, but if there was a face behind the windows today, the glare from the sun low in the western sky obscured them.

I went on down the stairs then, getting closer to the surf and its covering sounds. I'd had a satisfying day, and I was glad I'd showed up on the job as agreed, but the closer I got to home, the more uneasy I was about Crystal.

The sand scrunched under my feet, and I was tempted to take off my shoes and socks and wade part of the way. The tide was coming in, though, and I wasn't sure how much time I had to get around that rocky outcropping. It wasn't something I wanted to take a chance on. The alternative to the beach route was a very long hike home by the road if Crystal wouldn't drive over and get me, and I couldn't even imagine calling to ask her.

Just before I got to the rock, something made me turn and look back. There were only my own footprints

y

148

across the sand. And then I glanced up, to the top of the stairway.

A man stood there. A man in bib overalls.

He was just standing there, watching me. Bruce, who wasn't much of a conversationalist and who couldn't put gas in a lawn mower by himself.

Was there a sudden cool wind off the ocean, or was there another reason that a chill ran through me?

I suddenly remembered what Mr. Gyasi had said. *I hope Bruce didn't bother you.*

Did he have reason to think that might happen? And then he'd said, *If he bothers you, speak to either Mrs. Mallory or to me.*

I ran my hands over the goose bumps that had risen on my bare arms, staring up at Bruce. He just stood there, looking right at me, not self-conscious at being caught watching me.

I turned around suddenly and walked as fast as I could toward the point where the surf was nearly reaching the big rock. Bruce was a long way from me, so I didn't know why I was breathing so quickly, why I felt scared.

I didn't intend to turn around again, to check to see, at the last minute, if the man was still there. *I* was certainly self-conscious about being caught staring.

But then, at the last minute, I had to know.

He was still there, unmoving as one of the redwoods behind him. Watching me.

Watching me. I didn't know what Mr. Gyasi's definition of *bothering* was, but I knew it bothered me to have Bruce watching me. Yet how could I complain about something so simple as a man standing atop the cliff, looking down on me?

I turned and ran around the end of the rock, and didn't stop running until I reached our own stairway.

11

I dragged up the last few steps, puffing. Buster heard me and came to meet me, tail wagging, and the boys ran toward me, yelling a greeting.

"About time you got here! Crystal wouldn't let us go down to the beach," Sam said.

"Of course not. Dad said you couldn't go down alone." I was still blowing hard. "And I'm not up to another trip down there for a few minutes, either."

Buster was nosing about the sack I carried, and I opened it and unwrapped the uneaten sandwich, making his tail wag harder. He got it down in three bites.

"We waited all day, Nikki," Sam complained.

"Well, I worked all day," I informed him. I stood at

the top of our stairs and looked down, and as far north as I could see, but there was nobody on the beach. Bruce had only watched; he hadn't followed me.

I felt a bit foolish, now. Panicking that way. Just because the gardener, who maybe was kind of slow, mentally, had watched me.

"We fixed our own lunch," Jeremy informed me.

"Good. You're ten years old," I said. "That's old enough to make a sandwich."

Sam's face sobered. "I don't think Crystal is going to make any supper, either. Is she mad at all of us?"

"Probably just at me," I admitted. "She didn't want me to go to work, but Dad said I could, so I went. Did she say anything about it?"

"Not to us," Sam said. "What about supper? We are going to get something to eat eventually, aren't we?"

"I brought home some macaroni-and-cheese mixes when we went to the store last time. If Crystal doesn't cook, we can fix some of that. I guess I've got my wind back. Let's go down on the beach, but only for an hour, if I'm going to have to cook."

The boys tried to talk me into walking way up the beach, onto the shore below the Gyasi house, but I refused. It wasn't because I was afraid to go back there, I told myself. It just made more sense, for only an hour, to stay closer to home. Once Sam got over whining about my unwillingness to cooperate, he had a good time on our own beach.

The kids were right about Crystal and cooking. We didn't see anything of her, though when I went upstairs I heard her radio playing in her studio. We still had stuff for a salad, and when the macaroni and cheese was ready, I sent Sam up to tell Crystal it was ready; he came back with a message.

"She says she had a late lunch and isn't hungry now, but to save her a plateful and she'll reheat it later. Right now she's working."

So was that true, or was she simply not speaking to me? I hoped Dad wasn't going to be gone for much longer. And that reminded me to try once more to reach him by phone.

No answer at home. No answer at the office or on the cell phone. But just as we were clearing away the table, Crystal came downstairs, and the phone rang in the dining room, and when Sam answered it, it was Dad.

"He wants to talk to you," Sam said, offering the receiver to Crystal.

"Jeff?" Was there a note of panic in her voice. I was only a few feet from her, and it looked to me as if her knuckles were white, holding the receiver.

I shifted position uneasily, no longer so sure Dad

would back me up in disobeying her about going to work. I supposed I should move away and let her talk to him in private, but I was dying to know what was said.

"No, it's not," Crystal said, and my immediate guess was that he'd asked if everything was okay. I winced, and began to run water into the sink very slowly so that the sound of it didn't cover her voice. When Sam noisily set down his plate next to me on the counter, I gave him a dirty look and went, "Shh!"

"Jeff, I think I should pack up the kids and go home," Crystal said. "I can do that, just lock up the house here and—what? Jeff, listen—I really don't want to stay here, especially not without you."

So far she hadn't said *especially with a stepdaughter who defies me.* I held my breath, waiting for it.

I could tell by her face that Dad wasn't agreeing to her suggestion to go home. She said it again, "Jeff, listen—"

Obviously he wasn't listening; he was talking. When he did that to Mom, she had sometimes raised her voice and talked over his until he stopped. Crystal wasn't Mom. Crystal bit her lip, and I had the conviction that she was a hair away from crying. My guilt deepened, and I forced myself to look away from her, into the sudsy water where I was washing dishes.

"Please!" I heard her say, and then she listened some

more and turned her back to the rest of us and withdrew farther into the dining room. After that, though I heard the murmur of her voice, I couldn't make out the words.

And then I turned as she looked straight at me and held out the receiver. "He wants to talk to you," she said.

I braced myself and took the phone. Her hand, when it brushed mine, was ice cold. I wished I'd had a chance to get my side in first, before she'd told him whatever she'd told him. She was already picking up her plate and heading for the stairs without even heating it up. She was going to let me talk to him without listening in or interrupting.

"Uh, hi, Dad," I said. "When are you coming back?" Or had they already settled that, that we would all pack up and head north to Seattle?

"I don't know, honey. Ray's still in ICU at Harborview, in critical condition. The office is a mess because nobody has his power of attorney, or the authority to make decisions that need to be made. I'm hopeful that within a few more days he'll either take a turn for the better, or we can get the lawyers in and determine what it's possible for the rest of us to do. In the meantime, you guys hang in there and look after Crystal, okay?"

"We're not going home?" I said, not really surprised that Crystal hadn't swayed him.

"No, no, I'm sure I'll be able to get back to Trinidad within a matter of days. No sense spoiling everyone's vacation. Crystal seems sort of upset, but she'll be all right if you kind of take care of her, Nikki. Make things as easy for her as you can. I gather she still has several drawings to do, so take over everything else you can, okay?"

I opened my mouth to tell him my side of the story about going to work for Mr. Gyasi, then realized he hadn't said anything about that. Hadn't she told him?

"There's nothing wrong, is there?" Dad asked. "Everybody's okay?"

I was still in confession mode and couldn't quite believe I wasn't going to have to confess. "Um . . . well, Crystal had a bad nightmare the other night."

"Did she? Well, I'll be back with her as soon as I can. She wasn't still upset about the incident at the airport, was she?"

"Incident?" She hadn't mentioned any incident.

"That fellow who came up to her as we got there and spoke to her about her hair. I don't know why that should have been upsetting. Anybody who has gorgeous hair like that must encounter looks and comments, I should think."

"Some guy at the airport said something about her *hair?*"

"Said he'd only ever seen hair that color once before, many years ago, and that he'd never forgotten it. I was pretty taken with it myself, the first time I saw her, but of course I didn't comment on it. Not until I got to know her."

"Who was he?" I asked stupidly, having trouble getting onto this tangent after I'd prepared for a dressing-down in case he'd agreed with Crystal that I should not take the job.

"I don't know, just some older man who worked there, I think. I'm sure he didn't mean anything insulting. In fact, he thought it was beautiful, just different. She's sensitive, though, I'm sure you've realized that. And insecure. Try to keep her on an even keel until I get there."

"Sure," I said, feeling confused and almost numb. I had no idea how to do what he was asking of me.

"Sorry you couldn't get in touch me with sooner. I accidentally left the cell phone at the hospital when I was there; I'd loaned it to young Billock, and he put it down on his dad's bedside table, and he'd turned it off. I didn't notice it was missing until I'd gone home, too late at night to want to call down here then. I just got it back. While I was home, though, had a call from Bonnie, incidentally. She caught me the few minutes I was there, taking a shower."

Bonnie? Bonnie who belonged in a different world from the one I was in? "Is she okay?"

"She's having a blast," Dad said heartily in approval. He sounded so close, so big and strong and unafraid of anything that I wished desperately that he were here. To give me a hug, to reassure me that my life had not changed forever in a wrong direction, that things could still work out all right. "I gave her the phone number at the house in Trinidad, so she'll be calling you and filling you in on how much they're accomplishing, and how much fun it all is."

His tone changed subtly. "I'm sorry things aren't more fun for you right now, honey. I'll try to make it up to you when I get this mess cleared away here. And I'm concerned about Crystal. We're still on our honeymoon, after all, and I've abandoned her with a bunch of kids. She's never been around kids much; she was terrified even about meeting you, and I told her what a great family I have, that you'd all love her. I sure hope that's true, that all the people I love the most will like each other, at least. You'll try, won't you, Nikki?"

"Sure," I said. What else could I say? She hadn't told on me, I thought. And Dad hadn't asked about the job. She hadn't complained that I'd defied her and gone to work away from home, and I couldn't complain that she'd refused to drive me there. What was a twenty-minute walk on the beach instead of a ride?

Except, of course, for a few scary moments when a man in bib overalls stood watching me.

"I have to run," Dad said into my ear, and I wanted to reach out and touch him, hold him, not let him break contact. "You take care of everybody, honey. I'll see you in a few days."

And then he was gone, and there was nothing to do but replace the receiver.

"When Dad comes, can we go to the Humboldt State Marine Lab in Trinidad?" Sam demanded. "They've got all kinds of neat stuff there."

I stared at him. "How do you find out this stuff?"

"I listen. People at the store talk about things."

"When were you at the store when I wasn't? I didn't hear anybody talking about a marine lab."

"This afternoon."

I felt increasingly stupid. "You were in town at the store this afternoon?"

"Yeah. Crystal said she had to go in for a minute, and we couldn't stay here alone, so we went along."

"Crystal had to go to the store?" She couldn't take me to work—or wouldn't—but she'd gone into town? "Did she make you go inside?"

"No. I thought she would, because she looked funny, but she went in herself."

"How did she look funny?"

"She had a scarf over her head—a plain dark blue one—but not the way you do when you're out in the wind, just tied under your chin. She covered up her whole head, practically, and then wore these big dark glasses. Jeremy said probably people thought she was a celebrity in disguise."

In disguise? I remembered how the time she'd taken us in before, she'd worn a big hat with a wide brim. Who was she disguised as? Or from whom? She'd parked as far away from the door to the store as she could get.

"What did she go there for?"

He shrugged. "I don't know. She got something in a little bag. She didn't say what it was. I thought maybe she'd get some pork chops, or some hamburger, or something interesting to eat. Are we going to starve, Nikki, until Dad comes?"

"No, of course not." The things Dad had said kept chasing each other through my mind. Crystal was sensitive, insecure. She was supposed to still be on her honeymoon, but she was stuck with kids she didn't know very well, probably didn't like; she didn't know much about cooking; she undoubtedly missed Dad—I sucked in a deep breath. "Dad'll probably take you anywhere you want to go when he gets here," I predicted.

"Good. It's boring here if we can't go on the beach all day. That kid who works at the store, what's his name? Julian. That's a funny name, isn't it, for a boy? It sounds like a girl."

"A girl's name is Julia. Julian is a boy's name. What about him?"

"He's nice. He gave us each a fudge bar. The chocolate was cracked because somebody had dropped them, so he couldn't sell them. But they tasted okay. Why do those other guys pick on him? Keep calling him Spook and knocking over a rack of chips so he had to pick them up, and spilling pop on the floor so he had to mop it. They said it was an accident, but I don't think it was. Why do they act like that?"

"Because they're stupid," I said. "If Crystal takes you into town again tomorrow, suggest that she get something to make a meal out of. Something easy enough so even I can fix it. Even some frozen TV dinners, maybe."

"Fried chicken," Jeremy suggested.

"Yeah," Sam agreed. "Or Mexican. I like Mexican."

"Sam," Jeremy suggested, "let's go upstairs and play that new game."

"Okay," Sam said, but before they could get out of the kitchen I demanded, "What new game? Did Crystal buy you a game?"

"No, we found it in the attic. There's all kinds of stuff up there. A big box of games. Crystal said we could play with anything we found. She didn't know where the games came from. She said her Aunt Edna never played anything but Scrabble, but this one has all kinds of ships—cruisers, battleships, that kind of thing."

"I beat the first game," Jeremy said proudly, explaining why he was eager to try again.

I listened to them clattering up the stairs, jabbering away like crazy. Always before, I'd had Bonnie to talk to. I missed her like mad, I thought, swishing a glass through the sudsy water and rinsing it under the faucet.

I kept thinking about talking to Dad. Crystal hadn't told why she was mad at me, or even that she *was,* and he'd acted as if *I* were the grown-up and she was the child, and I should take care of her. How the heck could I do that? I wasn't ready to be the grown-up. I needed Bonnie. Or Mama. Oh, how I needed Mama!

Tears blurred my vision, and I wondered if you ever got over missing your mother after she was gone?

Certainly Crystal wasn't ever going to fill in for her.

I was just wiping my hands after draining the sink when the phone rang. I ran for the dining room and snatched it, flooded with relief when I heard my sister's voice. I expected her to sound far away, but she could have been as close by as Dad.

"Hey, Nickeroo!" She was laughing, and I heard other voices around her, in the background.

"You having a party?" I asked, already feeling better.

"Sort of. We just finished a house this afternoon, and the family is already moving into it. Father, mother, six kids, and a grandfather. All in this little dinky place no bigger than our living room and dining room at home. It's the first house they've ever owned, and they're so thrilled, and it makes us feel good, too. We're eating real Mexican food and listening to music and there's a pay phone in this place, so I wanted to talk to you."

"You haven't been answering my E-mail," I accused, forgiving her because she'd called now.

"No. I'm sorry, Nikki, there's been hardly any time, and besides, mostly there hasn't even been a place to plug in to electricity. It should be better when we leave for D.C. There'll be more places to plug in. How's it working out with Crystal? Dad sounds wonderfully happy with her."

"Well, that description doesn't exactly describe *my* relationship with her," I said flatly.

"Oh, Nick, aren't you even *trying,* for Dad's sake?"

"I *am,*" I stated. "But Dad had to leave without making it clear to her that he had said I could take this job, and—"

"You have a job?" Bonnie crowed. "That's terrific! Doing what?"

I told her.

"Well, I suppose if the guy were writing a romance novel, or a thriller, it might be more interesting typing, but it doesn't sound too bad. So what's the problem with Crystal?"

"I'm working in Mr. Gyasi's house, and it's about four miles by the road, and she refuses to drive me over."

"Do you have your bike there?"

"No. There wasn't room to bring bikes."

"So you're walking four miles each way? Bummer."

"Well, actually, it's closer by the beach, so I walked."

"So what's the problem?"

"When I told her I was going to work because Dad said I could, *she* said I couldn't. When the tide's in, I can't even get there by the beach. And I told her I was going anyway, and she hasn't spoken to me since. Except when she handed me the phone, when Dad called."

Bonnie sighed. "And I suppose you were completely undiplomatic when you told her you weren't going to follow her recommendation. As usual."

That stung.

"What do you mean, 'as usual'? Like I'm *always* undiplomatic? And she didn't give me a recommendation, she gave me an *order*. How diplomatic could I get? We couldn't get hold of Dad—he'd left his cell phone somewhere and it got turned off, and he wasn't at home or at the office when we were trying to call, so I didn't even have him to back me up—"

"What did he say when you finally talked to him?" Bonnie interrupted.

"Nothing. We didn't tell him."

"Even Crystal didn't tell him?"

"No. So I didn't mention it, either. It'll be easier to explain it all when he gets here."

"And in the meantime, you and Crystal aren't speaking to each other?"

"Oh, Bonnie, I have to go to the job. I really want the paycheck. Checks. Whatever. Crystal's . . . strange."

"She probably thinks you're strange, too. Dad said she's never been around kids, let alone teenagers." A teasing note crept back into her voice. "And you have to admit, Nick, you *are* weird, too."

"Thanks," I said stiffly.

"What does she do that's strange?" In the background, something crashed, and people laughed, but she was only momentarily distracted. "Somebody broke a glass. No great harm done. What about Crystal?"

"She has nightmares," I said.

"Lots of people have nightmares. They don't usually do it on purpose. You're not holding that against her, are you?"

"It was a really bad one. Scared her half to death. Even after she woke up—after I *woke* her up—she was cold and shaking. We went downstairs and had cocoa until she felt better."

"Well, that sounds more encouraging. I don't see how you're getting *strange* out of this, Nick."

"She refuses to leave the house without"—I hesitated—"without being in disguise."

"In disguise? What are you talking about?"

"She covers up her head, so you can't see her hair. She wears big sunglasses."

"Oh, for Pete's sake, Nikki! It's summer! The sun is bright!"

"Dad said there was an incident at the airport," I told her stubbornly, feeling somewhat foolish yet also very uneasy. "Some man commented on her hair, and it upset her."

"She has beautiful hair! Lots of people would notice it, I think," Bonnie said. "That silvery white, almost. Hardly anybody has hair like that."

"I think that's what the man at the airport said. He'd only seen hair like that once before, or something like that. He was admiring it, Dad said, not insulting her, but he said she's sensitive. Why would having beautiful hair make you sensitive?"

"I can't imagine. Who was this guy? Somebody she knew?"

"No. A stranger. Dad thought maybe he worked at the airport. She didn't know him."

"That's a really small airport, isn't it? Maybe you should go over there and see if you can find him and ask him what he meant by his comment." She sounded half-serious.

"Oh, sure! It's too far to walk, so I should ask Crystal if she'll drive me over there so I can find the guy who upset her by saying she had pretty hair, or whatever it was. Right, Bonnie."

"Well, I think you're making a mountain out of a molehill. Give her a break, Nikki. If Dad says she's sensitive, she's probably having a terrible time adjusting to just being married, let alone to being around his kids. She's heard all the stories about mouthy teenagers—"

"I'm not a mouthy teenager!" I objected. "Give *me* a

break, Bonnie! All I wanted was to take this job, have a chance to earn a little money while I'm here, and she didn't have any *reason* to tell me I couldn't do it! No reason to say she wouldn't drive me over there so I wouldn't have to walk!"

"Maybe," Bonnie said, laughing, "she just doesn't want to be seen by anyone who might recognize her. Or comment on her silvery hair!"

"Maybe you're right," I said, but I wasn't laughing. "If you were here, it would be giving you the creeps too."

"The creeps? What's to have the creeps about? She covers up her hair, she retreats to her studio to work—Dad said she was finishing up a job for B&B—and doesn't know how to relate to kids. That's creepy?"

"Well, no. That part isn't creepy. And I'm probably being silly about that." I told her about Bruce, in his bib overalls, watching me from the top of the cliff."

"Oh, Nick," Bonnie said, against a background of laughter, "I think you're suffering from puberty. At fourteen, you're not grown up yet, but you're not a little kid, either, and you're missing Mom—and me—and now Dad's gone too, and you just need some time to adjust to this new marriage and everything."

"Everything's out of kilter, somehow," I said, suddenly feeling close to tears at the unexpected lack of support from my sister. "I wish you were here, Bon."

"Well, I'm sorry I'm not. But things will work out. Just hang in there. Listen, I need to go calm down this wild bunch of celebrating Christian house-builders. Just hang in, okay?"

I didn't even get to say *okay,* and she was gone.

Later, I'd wish she'd called the next day, so that I could have told her what Crystal did next. Even Bonnie would have had to admit *that* was weird.

12

This time, I knew at once what I was hearing.

I'd left my bedroom window open to the sounds of the surf below. When I'd gone to sleep, Jeremy and Sam had still been giggling down the hall. I figured if they were bothering Crystal, she could tell them to shut up and go to sleep. And then I felt guilty, because what if she didn't feel she could do that? Dad wouldn't have hesitated a minute, but Crystal was intimidated by kids.

Anyway, the ocean sounds were soothing, and Buster was warm against my back, and I slept soundly after a few minutes of hoping that Bruce wouldn't be there watching me from the top of the stairs the next day.

I woke, again in pitch darkness, and heard her.

Another nightmare.

Nightmares aren't usually fatal, are they? Was it my responsibility to wake her up? Or would she wake up on her own if I left her alone?

Take care of everybody, Dad had said. And that especially included Crystal.

I would count to one hundred, I decided, running my fingers through Buster's warm fur. If she was still making those horrific noises then, I'd go wake her up. I doubted that she'd want to go downstairs with me for cocoa, though. It was hard to know what to say to someone who wasn't speaking to you.

Ninety-eight, ninety-nine, one hundred.

I wished I were getting deaf, like poor old Buster, because all too clearly I heard the moan that came from a tortured throat, a cry of pure terror.

I hadn't had a nightmare in ages. The last time, before Mom got sick, she'd come in and sat on the edge of my bed, and brushed the hair back from my forehead, and talked to me until I calmed down.

If Dad were here, he'd be in there with her. Putting his arms around her. Speaking soothing words.

Dad wasn't here. I was.

I got out of bed, feeling the cold floor beneath my bare feet, and padded along the hallway. This time I flicked on the switch so that the hall was illuminated, very softly. The light didn't penetrate very far into Crystal's room when I gently nudged the door open.

"Crystal? You're having a bad dream again."

The moan was cut off before it could become a shriek, and even though I knew she was only dreaming, I shivered, remembering how it felt to be trapped in terror from which there was no escape except waking.

She gasped, and sat up. I could tell that much in the dim light. There was something not quite right about her, but I couldn't grasp what it was.

"Crystal?" My hand crept out toward the light switch, but she protested, immediately.

"No! Don't turn on the light! I'm awake now! I'm sorry I disturbed you."

"It's okay," I said, though it wasn't. "Do you want me to get you anything?"

"No. No, wait. Would you mind looking in the top drawer of the dresser? You won't need a light. There's a nightgown on the right-hand side, right on top. I think I need a dry one, please."

I didn't see what the big deal was about the light, but I made my way to the dresser and groped for the gown. I recognized it by the feel of the lace. One of her bridal nighties; I'd seen it when she was packing.

I approached the bed and handed it over. She waited until I'd turned away to strip off the one that must have been soaked in sweat. I was back in bed before I realized what had not seemed right.

The other time I'd awakened her, I'd seen her silvery hair, luminescent even in the near darkness. Tonight, I hadn't.

Was she even covering up her hair when she went to bed?

What sense did that make?

What if Dad had married a woman who was truly unbalanced?

He hadn't known her very long. He'd never met any of her family, what little family she admitted to having. How much else was there he didn't know about her?

What if he'd left the boys and me here alone with a woman who was seriously unstable?

Then, reason reasserted itself. I could imagine what my sister would say: *Give her a break, Nick.*

I curled around Buster until I got warm again, and went to sleep.

An enveloping fog had come in overnight.

It made it cool enough so that I put a sweater over my short-sleeved shirt, and I wore socks. I wondered if they'd feed me breakfast if I got there while Julian was having his, and decided I'd better not risk it. Cold cereal was safer than missing breakfast altogether.

It was eerie, starting down the stairs into that fog. It was damp against my face and my hair, and so thick, I could only see a few steps below me, so I clung to the railing. I'd gone down quite a ways—I couldn't tell how far I was from the bottom, maybe halfway?—when I realized that Buster was on my heels.

I stopped, exasperated. "What are you doing here?" It was my own fault, of course. He'd come downstairs with me and asked to go out, and I'd forgotten to call him back inside before I left.

He leaned into me and wagged his tail.

"You can't come, Buster. Go home!"

He smiled at me. Other people laughed when I said my dog smiled, but he *did*.

"Stay, Buster! You can't go with me!"

He licked my outstretched hand.

I looked upward, trying to judge how far I'd come, how long it would take to drag him home and shut him in the house, and then come down again.

I couldn't see the top of the stairs. I couldn't see the bottom. I couldn't see anything but a couple of steps above and below, and the railing at my side. The surf sounded loud, close. I ought to have allowed extra time to get there in this murk, but I hadn't.

If I went up again with Buster, I'd be late for work. I

did not think Mr. Gyasi dealt kindly with employees who were late.

"All right," I said finally, starting down, "you'll have to come with me. You'll probably have to stay on their porch all day. With nothing to eat."

Buster wagged his tail some more, and stuck to my heels.

I had never been in fog so thick. I could hardly get lost, with the booming surf to my left, and the cliff at my right, so I forged ahead, suddenly grateful for the dog now trotting at my side.

We rounded the projecting rock, and now I kept close to the base of the cliff, not wanting to miss the stairs to the green house. For a few panicky minutes I thought I must have missed them, because it took longer than I thought it ought to, and then they were there.

I gasped audibly in relief, and made one more try at sending Buster home. He wagged his tail and licked my hand, and I started up the stairs. The dog was close enough behind me to give me a nudge once in awhile, and I was glad he'd refused to leave me.

I emerged at last at the top, vowing that if fog was going to be a factor, I'd allow an extra half hour next time. The house loomed over us, and I hurried toward its welcoming lights. And then, with no warning, the lights were blocked out and I ran solidly into the man who obscured them.

We both let out grunts, and Bruce's rusty-sounding voice said, "Sorry. Sorry."

If it had been anyone but Bruce, I'd have been glad to see him. As it was, I felt the way Crystal must have felt during the nightmare, with my heart pounding uncomfortably.

"Excuse me," I choked, and started to move around him, and he said, "Dog."

"Yes. His name's Buster. He followed me and I couldn't make him go home."

"Buster," Bruce said. I didn't linger to talk to him but dashed for the house.

I rang the bell, an old-fashioned nonelectrical one you operated by twisting; it was set into the door itself, and Julian opened it a moment later.

"You don't have to ring. Just walk in," he greeted me. "Don't you love that fog?"

I didn't know whether he was kidding or not. "It's pretty thick," I said.

"Like being in the world all by yourself," Julian observed, and sounded as if he wouldn't mind being out in it.

"I don't want to be in the world all by myself," I said, still shivering even though the house was warm.

Julian laughed. "Well, not permanently and full-time. But once in awhile it's great. You want to hang your sweater up here, or keep it on?"

"I think I'll wear it for a while," I decided. "Um—my dog followed me. I couldn't make him go home. Is it okay if he stays on the porch?"

"You can bring him inside with you, if you want," he said. "Everybody here likes dogs. Even Dad." He reopened the front door and said, "Come on in, dog."

"His name's Buster. He's fourteen years old, same as I am, and he's getting deaf, but he's a nice old dog."

Buster willingly followed me inside, tail wagging. He sniffed investigatively at Julian's outstretched hand, then licked it.

"You've been approved," I told him.

"Well, come on out in the kitchen, Buster. We're about to have pancakes and sausage. Thank heaven we don't have to eat what Dad does. His glop wouldn't tempt a starving Arab off the desert." He led the way down the hall toward the kitchen, from which mouth-watering aromas drifted toward us.

"Does he have a bad stomach?" I asked, following.

"Yeah. An ulcer, I guess. Nothing agrees with him. His stomach's always upset. It doesn't help his disposition. Here, Buster, you can lie down right there, on that rug, and Nikki, you can sit at the end of the table."

I didn't argue this time. It smelled too good, and my cold cereal was long gone. The kitchen was warm, and the food that was set before me looked like a big improvement over cornflakes. Buster, nose lifted, quivered a little as he obediently sank onto the rag rug.

Mrs. Mallory regarded him with acceptance. "Been a long time since we had a dog around here," she said. "He's smelling that sausage, but it's not that good for him, so I'll only give him a little taste. Pancakes aren't too bad."

"I ran into Bruce out there in the fog," I said, accepting maple syrup to pour over the stack of three that I'd been provided. "Literally. We didn't see each other until we collided."

"Comparing fog to pea soup isn't too far off," Julian observed, slathering butter on his hotcakes before reaching for the syrup pitcher. "It can be like being blind."

"He watched me yesterday when I left," I said. "He stood at the top of the stairs as long as I was in sight."

Julian hesitated with a forkful halfway to his mouth. "Is he bothering you?"

"He hasn't *done* anything," I had to admit. "Except watch me. I'm not exactly comfortable with being watched."

Unexpectedly, he laughed. "Well, you'd better get used to it. Guys are going to be watching you from now on."

Uncertainly, I searched his face. "What do you mean by that?"

"Don't you look in a mirror? You're a pretty girl, Nikki. Guys look at pretty girls."

The compliment took me totally off guard. "But he's an old man! Well, he must be in his forties or more, isn't he?"

"You think old men—or men in their forties—don't look at pretty girls?" He was still grinning. "Even Dad does, when he thinks nobody's noticing. Age has nothing to do with it."

Ruefully, I nodded. "My dad certainly looked. He just married a woman almost young enough to be one of his daughters. Crystal, her name is."

"The one who inherited the house. Did she use to live around here?"

"I don't know where she lived before her parents were killed in an accident. She came to the house where we're staying when she was seven, to live with her aunt until she was adopted into a family."

Julian cut off a piece of pancake, made sure it wasn't dripping, and tossed it to Buster, who swallowed it so fast, he couldn't possibly have tasted it. "I just wondered. She was in the store yesterday for a few minutes. One of our customers saw her and asked about her. Said she reminded him of somebody, maybe, but he couldn't think who."

Thinking about Crystal made me uncomfortable. Made me feel guilty. *Take care of her,* Dad had said. How did I do it? Especially when I didn't really want the responsibility?

"This is delicious," I said to Mrs. Mallory, and she smiled. "Do you ever feel that growing up is more painful than it ought to be?"

"Absolutely," Julian said. "Dad says it's just the way life is. A lot of things hurt, and it doesn't get any easier because you've reached twenty, or forty, or fifty. He was forty-seven when my mom got killed, in the same accident that crippled him. I think losing her was harder on him than the injuries. It made him give up the teaching he'd always loved. I was surprised he finally came out of the grief enough to tackle this book he'd been talking about doing for years. I thought he was going to come back here, to this house where he grew up and lived until he went off to college and then to work down in the valley, and just be a vegetable the rest of his life. He admits that can happen when a man loses his wife and everything that means anything to him."

"I guess that's what happened to my dad, too. He lost Mom—she was sick for more than a year before she died—and he sort of lost his bearings. He still had us kids, but we weren't enough."

For a moment, our eyes held, sharing that knowledge. "It hurts, not to be enough," I said in a low voice.

"Yeah. But it's understandable, too, that a man loved his wife enough so he can't adjust to being without her. My dad is finally beginning to adjust a little bit, writing this book. I hope something worthwhile comes of it, that it finds a publisher, that people like it and buy it. I don't think he'll ever get married again, not being in the wheelchair the way he is. But your dad found someone else to help make his life bearable."

Bearable. Is that what it was, with Crystal? How could I deny him that? If he couldn't be wildly happy, the way he was with Mom before they knew she was dying, could he at least find life bearable?

My eyes stung, and I devoted myself to the pancakes and sausage, saving the last bite for Buster. "I'd better get to work, or your dad will kick me out."

"I don't think so. He's grateful that somebody's doing the part he can't do, one-handed. And he's baffled by computers, even if he had both hands that worked."

"Computers are easy to learn," I stated, pushing back my chair.

"For someone your age," Mrs. Mallory said wryly,

coming to clear the table. "Not so easy for someone older. Finish the job, young lady. Mr. Gyasi's in a better mood since he knows it's going to be done."

It was hard to tell, I thought later when my employer came to check on my progress. He seemed as gruff and reserved as he had initially. While he was looking through the pages I'd printed out so far this morning as the fog pressed in around the windows, I saw him pop one of those antacid tablets into his mouth. I could smell the minty odor.

I spoke without considering my words ahead of time, just the way Bonnie says I usually do. "My stepmother drinks raw carrot juice every day. I think it soothes her stomach."

He paused, looking away from the sheaf of papers in his hand. "Carrot juice?"

"She even brought the juicer with us from home, so she could fix it fresh every morning. Dad says it's pretty good if you grind up an apple with it."

He regarded me in a way I couldn't interpret. "And it soothes her stomach?"

"I think so."

"Hmm. Here's another typographical error." He extended the page for me to see.

"*That* instead of *than*," I read. "Another one the spell-checker couldn't catch because they're both real words. I'll fix it."

I remembered Buster, then, lying quietly beside me. "My dog followed me this morning. Julian thought it would be all right if he stayed in here with me."

"Yes, he told me. No problem. I'm sorry we don't have a rug for him to lie on in here. We don't have any in the rooms where I have to move around with my chair; it doesn't do well over throw rugs. Your dog looks rather elderly. You've had him a long time."

"They got him when I was a few months old, so he's fourteen," I said. Buster knew we were talking about him; he lifted his head so I could scratch behind his ears.

"Is that all you are? Fourteen?" He stared at me and for a moment I feared he was going to say I was too young for the job. "Hmm. I'd assumed you were older." He adjusted the position of his chair fractionally and dropped his good hand down so that Buster could lick it, then wheeled completely and left the room with no further comment.

He'd thought I was older. And Julian thought that guys would be looking at me from now on. He'd said I was a pretty girl.

Well, I hadn't exactly thought I was *ugly*. But Julian was the first boy to tell me I was pretty.

It put me in a good mood to get back to work, and to look for the typos on my own before Mr. Gyasi found them.

The time had passed quickly when Julian stuck his head around the corner of the door. "Break time! Actually, it's almost noon, but Mrs. Mallory says we have time for a house tour before lunch comes out of the oven. Chicken pot pie. Even Dad may be able to eat a little of it."

I let the screen saver take over on the computer and got to my feet. "Is it still too foggy to see anything outside?"

"Pretty much, but I'll show you the inside. Want Buster to come?"

I wasn't sure I had a choice about that. Buster was going to stick to my heels today, in this unfamiliar house.

We climbed stairs first, starting at the top. On the second floor level, high up because of those fourteen-foot ceilings, Julian paused. "You want to see the tower, too?"

"Yes, of course. We've got a tower, but it's nothing like yours. I'd love to see it."

So we climbed past the attic level—nothing worth seeing in there, though there was some junk stored there, Julian said—and high into that tower room.

It was bigger than ours, and furnished. There was a

single bed, and a dresser, and a small table with one chair. There was also a rocker with flowered cushions.

Beyond the windows on all four walls, sunlight filtered through the fog, but not enough of it to increase visibility very much. We couldn't see the ocean, only the tops of the nearest trees. It was like being suspended in space, a bit eerie, but restful. "Does someone live up here?" I asked. For some reason, I didn't think it was Julian's room.

"Yeah, Bruce does. He likes being up here on his own. Dad can't get above the first floor, so he doesn't care what we do with the rest of it. I guess he lived up here for a while when he was a kid."

Knowing that this was Bruce's bed, Bruce's rocking chair, made it different somehow. Chilling, though why should that be? There was nothing personal about it, no belongings scattered around, very neat. Almost institutional.

I wasn't sorry to go back down, only regretful that the fog made it impossible to see the ocean, and maybe our house. If we could see their tower, surely they could see ours. That must have been Bruce I'd spotted that day in the window here. Had he known we were watching him? How did it feel to be the watched, instead of the watcher?

I lost track of how many bedrooms there were on

the second floor. They were all furnished, as if waiting for guests who would never come—or were simply long gone in the first place. There were pictures on the walls here, and a 1971 calendar, open to the month of September. What had happened in September of 1971 that had made the occupant of this room stop turning the pages of his or her calendar?

I posed the question aloud, and Julian shrugged. He didn't know either.

"This next one's mine," he said. "I'm kind of glad Bruce wanted the tower room. I like having this entire floor to myself."

I slanted a glance at him. "I'm getting the impression you'd like to be a hermit."

He laughed. "It would have its advantages. I made the bed, in your honor. I don't usually bother."

Immediately I knew that this room would have been my choice too. It was big, as was every room in the house, and it faced the Pacific. Today, though the fog was finally thinning, the water was slate colored instead of blue, but from here you would ordinarily be able to see freighters plying the coast, and small fishing boats and an occasional sailboat.

When the storms came in—and they would—you'd see the rising swells and feel the wind shaking this old glass—there were colored panes in some of them, the originals from when the house was built, I was sure—

because it hadn't been updated to double panes like Aunt Edna's house.

And I would have known this was Julian's room. How had I guessed that he would have cases spilling books all over everything? And a guitar, and a desk with a workmanlike lamp, and pictures of sailing ships and one of the sun slanting through the redwoods, just the way we'd observed it while driving through them.

It was neither messy nor overly neat. There was an old-fashioned and colorful quilt on the double bed, with some extra pillows for late-night reading. No rocker here, but a padded window seat looking out to sea, with a book open on the cushion, as if he'd just been interrupted. I walked over to look at the cover, and smiled.

"I love the *Vorkosigan* books too."

"If I were going to be a writer," Julian said, "that's the kind of book I'd want to write. The way Lois McMaster Bujold writes."

For just a moment I knew what it was like to meet a kindred soul.

It was strange, and wonderful, and though it was sort of overpowering, I had no inclination to back away from it. Somehow I knew, instinctively, that this was one of the parts of growing up that other people found satisfying even while it was, in its own way, terrifying.

Had Dad felt this way, when he'd met Crystal?

And then we heard Mrs. Mallory calling up the stairway: "Lunch is ready!"

The tour was over. "I'd like to see it again when the sun's shining," I said as we walked side by side down the wide stairway.

The chicken pot pie was so wonderful, I asked if the recipe was a secret, and Mrs. Mallory laughed. "Heavens, no! A cook, are you?"

"Not yet, but I'd better learn before we all starve. My stepmother knows even less than I do," I said, and didn't add that she wasn't speaking to me, either, so it was hard for either of us to learn much of anything.

"It's very easy," Mrs. Mallory said. "I'll write it down for you."

Julian went to work after lunch, and Buster had some of the pot pie—sacrilege, my dad would have called it, to feed such ambrosia to a dog, though Dad had spoiled him over the years too—and when it was four o'clock, I tucked the recipe into my pocket, patted my leg to summon Buster, and headed for home.

The fog still drifted around me, but it had lifted enough so that I could see the stairs all the way to the bottom. When I looked back from the bottom, there was no sign of a watcher up above, nor when I paused while rounding the rocky barricade. Somehow, with Buster along, it didn't matter so much.

The boys were sitting at the kitchen table, playing a board game. There were empty bags and wrappers at their elbows. "What's for supper?" Sam asked as soon as I came in the door.

"Good afternoon to you, too," I said cheerfully. I was still basking in what had been a fairly delightful day.

"We haven't seen Crystal all day except when she came down to get a sandwich at noon. She had some kind of funny hat on again," Sam informed me.

"Even in the house?"

"It wasn't exactly a hat," Jeremy corrected. "It was sort of a scarfy thing, tied like this." He gestured to indicate how all-enveloping it had been.

Give her a break, Nikki, I thought. If Dad thought she was normal, maybe she was. I determined to try not to think about it. Sooner or later he'd figure it out for himself if he stuck around home long enough.

I went to the cupboard where Aunt Edna had stored her supplies. "I thought I saw some canned chicken in here. And I know there was a bag of mixed vegetables in the freezer. Now if I just locate some biscuit mix—ah! I think I have all the ingredients for chicken pot pie!"

The boys were cheered up at the thought that I was actually going to prepare something to eat, though by the quantity of wrappers around them, they could hardly be starving.

I heard her coming down the stairs, and deliberately didn't turn to look. I set out measuring cups and milk and found a baking pan, and was reaching for a mixing bowl when I heard Sam suck in his breath behind me.

I turned and the bowl slid out of my hand to smash on the floor. I scarcely felt the glass splinters spatter over my feet and ankles.

"Holy cow!" Sam said, his mouth sagging open. "Dad's going to kill you!"

For once he wasn't saying that to me. He was speaking to Crystal, whose beautiful silvery hair was now a drab, ugly brown.

13

No wonder there had been something peculiar about her in the middle of the night. No wonder she'd been covering her hair.

She was looking at Sam when he spoke, and all the blood left her face. She put out a hand to the door frame, and then turned and ran. Back up the stairs. Slamming her bedroom door.

Sam and Jeremy regarded me in amazement. "Why on earth did she do that?" Sam demanded.

I had no idea. Or did I? Hiding? In disguise?

Why else would you dye beautiful hair to the color of mud?

Oh, Dad, what have you gotten yourself into?

Take care of her, he'd told me. Did that include keeping her from ruining her hair?

"Nikki, you're bleeding," Jeremy told me.

I looked down to see the red flecks on my socks. "Get me the broom and the dustpan," I said, and stooped to begin picking up the larger pieces.

"Maybe," Jeremy said, sounding subdued, "she thinks you meant it, Sam. That your dad will really kill her."

Sam brought me the broom and dustpan, dismay on his face. "She couldn't truly believe that, could she, Nikki?"

"Of course not," I said, sweeping up the rest of the glass. But I remembered what she'd said after that first nightmare—something about they were all dead, and there was blood all over everything. *That dream couldn't have been based on anything she'd actually known about, could it?*

There was no sound from upstairs. I didn't want to go up there. I didn't want to talk to Crystal. Yet he'd told me to take care of her.

I dumped the broken glass into the trash can and went to the phone and called the number of Dad's cell phone. No answer, which probably meant that he was in a meeting or somewhere he had to turn it off for a while. Calling our house at home produced no reply, either.

For a moment I was furious with him. It was his

responsibility to be here, to figure out whatever was the matter with his new wife, to take care of it.

Yet it was also his responsibility to take care of the crisis at work. It was part of his job. Part of a job he loved, most of the time.

Part of being a grown-up.

"Are we going down to the beach?" Sam asked when I gave up with the phone.

"Are we going to get anything to eat?" Jeremy wondered.

"Yes to food, sooner or later. No to the beach. It's too cold and foggy down there right now, anyway," I decided. And then, reluctantly, I said, "I guess I'd better go up and talk to her."

I'd rather have taken poison.

It was all I could do to climb the stairs. Buster, clearly sensing that something was wrong, padded along behind me.

Crystal's door was closed. I tapped on it, and then when she didn't answer, I eased it open and peered in.

She was sitting on the bed. The mud-colored hair was grotesque, ugly. She put up her hands and ran them through it as if she wanted to tear it out. She had turned on her bedside light, and I saw the shine of tears on her cheeks.

How many times had I felt ugly and scared and

inadequate? Buster nudged my hand in sympathy, and I couldn't help but feel a twinge of my own. Crystal looked so pathetic.

I didn't know for sure what Dad would say to her now, but if I were in her place, I'd want somebody to give me a hug and tell me things weren't as bad as I thought they were, even if they *were* that bad.

I couldn't go across the room and hug her. Not even Dad could expect me to do that.

"Sam didn't mean it literally," I said after a long moment when we just looked at each other. "Dad will be . . . shocked . . . but he won't *kill* you. He might kill me if I don't do something about . . . whatever's wrong here."

There was a fresh gush of tears, and she wiped them away with the back of one hand. I walked over to her dresser and opened a drawer, poking around until I found a handkerchief, and carried it to her.

She blew her nose. "I hope he won't kill either one of us," she said through a plugged-up nose.

"Why did you do it? You have such beautiful hair." I was close to her now, looking down on her. "Dad loves your hair." I swallowed and felt compelled to add, "He loves you."

That didn't seem to help. She crumpled up the

handkerchief and swiped again at her face. "He'll never forgive me," she said.

"For what? Dyeing your hair mud brown? I remember one time when Mom tried a red tint, and he hated it, but it grew out. They didn't get a divorce over it. Yours will grow out too." I studied it for a moment. "Maybe— maybe you could add just a tint of—blond, or auburn, or something. So it wouldn't be so—"

"So ugly," she said.

"If you think it's ugly, why did you do it? Was it because some stranger at the airport commented on your hair? He *was* a stranger, wasn't he?"

For long seconds she stared at me, then said so softly that I could hardly hear her, "He remembered."

"Remembered what?"

"Remembered it all. The story from all those years ago. He probably saw me as a child, with unusual hair— it was in all the papers, that I had almost totally white hair—and he was startled to see it again."

I was beginning to feel seriously uneasy. And she was twisting her head to look up at me. I pulled over a chair and sat down facing her. "Those nightmares you've been having, are they about something that really happened? When you were a little kid?"

"I should have told Jeff," she said miserably. "I knew

it wasn't right to marry him without telling him. But I . . . couldn't."

"You said . . . everybody was dead," I remembered. "And that there was blood all over everything. Did you see something like that?"

She had drenched the handkerchief, and I got up and brought her the entire stack in the dresser drawer. I wasn't sure she was going to answer me. She wasn't meeting my gaze anymore, but staring blankly across the room.

"I was the only one left alive in the entire house," she said finally.

The hairs rose on the back of my neck and on my arms. I couldn't make my voice work to ask the next question for too long a time, during which she sat there silently with tears dripping off her face and spotting her blue shirt.

"You found them?" I finally managed, and nobody would have recognized my voice. "Your parents? Is that how they died? Not in an accident—"

"I was in bed, asleep, when I heard them," she said, and now it was as if she'd gone into a trance. "I came down the stairs and found them. The knife was still there, dropped in the middle of the living room, covered with . . . I was only seven, but I knew how to call the police."

She came out of it then, and looked directly at me, and there was a new firmness in her voice, in her look. "You're working for the Gyasis, aren't you? In the next house up the beach?"

Startled, I almost choked. "What do they have to do with anything?"

"I didn't realize it at first, not until today when I asked where you'd gone, and Sam said to work, next door. I didn't want to take you to work because after the man at the airport remembered that the child who'd discovered those murders had been a platinum blonde, I didn't want to be seen by anyone else who might remember. It was over twenty years ago, but there are still people living in Humboldt County who will remember the story. So I covered up my hair. It was the only way anyone could realize who I was. Only I didn't figure it out until Sam told me you had *walked*. There was only one place near enough for you to have walked."

I felt as if I were encased in a block of ice. My wrists and my ankles were so cold, they ached. My mouth was dry and my heart was thudding painfully as I waited for her to say it, the unthinkable, the impossible.

"It was in that house that it happened," Crystal said. "Where I was visiting with my parents at my grand-parents' house when I was a little girl."

14

"Are you related to the Gyasi family?" I asked, trying to control the tremors that kept running through me.

"I think the one living there now must be my uncle. His name was Hudson. I don't remember him. He was away somewhere, down in the central valley, when it happened. He and I were the only ones who survived the attack—he because he wasn't there, and I because Cecil didn't realize I was upstairs. Or maybe he wouldn't have cared about one little girl, since I wasn't with the others when it happened."

The ache in my throat made it hard to swallow. "Did they find out who did it?"

"Oh, there never was any question about that," Crystal said, and now that she'd begun to let the dam break, she was calmer, though she, too, was shaking visibly. "He was Hudson's younger brother. Cecil B. Gyasi." She said that as if she were reading it from a newspaper.

The worm of dread formed in the pit of my stomach, writhing there. Cecil *B.* Gyasi? Did the *B* stand for *Bruce*?

"He'd never been normal," Crystal was saying. "He'd had temper tantrums from the time he was a teenager. Destructive ones, when he broke windows and set fires and hit people. Once, he killed a dog. The family knew he was sick, and they tried to get help, but nothing anyone tried helped at all. He ought to have been locked up, but they thought they could manage him at home—they even hired an attendant who had worked in a mental hospital to live at the house to try to keep him under control; his name was Paul—but Paul had been called home to Sacramento on a family emergency that night."

Her throat moved convulsively. "Nobody survived to tell what had set him off. We don't know why he took that big knife and . . . did what he did. He wouldn't talk about it afterward, to the police or to the psychiatrists. They said he wasn't capable of contributing to his own defense, and there wasn't even a trial, just a hearing when they put him in a mental institution."

I was recalling, with alarming clarity, that room in the tower of the green Victorian, the room that even then I had thought seemed institutional, like a room kept by someone who had lived apart from society. In a prison, perhaps, or a mental institution.

I felt as if I were suffocating, yet I kept my eyes fixed on Crystal's. Her mouth quavered, ever so slightly, as she attempted a parody of a smile.

"Did you ever think what it must be like for the families of serial killers? Mass murderers? Whether or not the people they killed were their own relatives?"

I had, actually. While Mom was so sick, we watched TV more than we would have otherwise. We tried to stay away from news shows, because they were so depressing, but there was a period when there was no getting away from hearing about the Walcott case. Emory Walcott had been a serial killer in the Puget Sound area, and his family had been the ones who'd discovered the initial evidence and turned him in. He had a wife and seven kids, who had considered him an ideal husband and father, until they came across appalling evidence that a body had been transported in the family van.

"How terrible for them," Mom had said softly. "Imagine, someone you loved being responsible for something like that."

Crystal was doubly a victim. Her family had been murdered, and her uncle had been the perpetrator.

She hadn't expected me to respond to her question,

and she went on speaking. "I can tell you what it's like, being the one who survived. Even after I was adopted and taken away from here, and even though I never told a soul about any of it, not even the counselors and psychiatrists they brought to talk to me, somebody always found out. No matter how often we moved, no matter how many times I changed schools, someone always discovered who I was. A timid little big-eyed girl who was afraid of everything. Who never had nerve enough to make a friend. Who cried when she was teased or ridiculed. Children can be very cruel, you know. That's why I'm still . . . afraid of children."

"You were afraid to marry Dad because of *us?*"

Her face under the muddy hair crumpled, and the tears, which had momentarily trickled off, began to seep down her face again. "I was afraid of everybody. I hid in books and in my drawing. I won a contest—I was actually brave enough to enter a contest, because I thought it would be completely anonymous—and I won a scholarship to an art school, and a few people saw my drawings and liked them. I didn't have to meet the public, I simply turned over my work to a dealer who showed them, and I began to sell a few. And then I met Mr. Brandbury of B&B, and he liked my work, and I was able to quit my job in an office and just *draw,* the way I'd already dreamed of doing."

Buster was leaning against my leg, warm and hard, and I put out a hand to scratch behind his ears. How do dogs know when you're stressed out? How do they know you need their comfort? I welcomed his warmth, his affection, as blindly as it was offered.

"I thought I could be reasonably contented that way," Crystal went on. "Living alone, earning a living with my art, so I didn't have to encounter people. And then I met Jeff, when I went into B&B's office to deliver some of my sketches. I had no intention of getting better acquainted with him, with any of them. I just needed to earn a living, and I had to deliver the drawings and have consultations with the art director and the editor of the book I was to illustrate. Jeff saw me, and he was friendly and helpful, and when he asked me out, I was afraid to go, at first. He was so gentle, though, almost as if he'd guessed how wounded I was, and so funny, yet so—"

"Pushy?" I supplied, and incredibly, we both laughed a little.

"Pushy," Crystal agreed. "He wouldn't take no for an answer. I wouldn't go to him, but he insisted on coming to me. He told me how lonely he was, about losing your mother, and he just wouldn't go away. And when he asked me to marry him—" She drew in a deep breath, and I realized I needed to inhale more deeply, too, before I was so oxygen-starved, I passed out.

"Can you imagine what that was like, Nikki?" she asked earnestly. "After all those lonely years, of adoptive parents who couldn't stand the strain of having a daughter who was part of the infamous Gyasi murder case, who made me so uncomfortable with *their* discomfort that I finally severed the relationship altogether. I think they always wondered if that same wild, dangerous streak was in my genes, that I might suddenly turn on them and ..."

She couldn't put that part of it into words, and she paused for breath. "And then there was Jeff. He didn't treat me as if I were the survivor of a horrible massacre, or had bad genes that might surface to destroy anything and everything around me. He treated me like a *woman*, a desirable *woman*, in need of love and comfort, the same as himself."

She looked deeply into my face then. "Do you know what a wonderful man your father is, Nikki?"

I did. I remembered all the tender loving things he'd done during the last year of Mom's life. The way he'd come home with funny stories to make her laugh. The way he'd sat beside her bed and held her hand for hours at a time during the final days.

My throat ached something awful, and I couldn't reply.

"I knew if I told him," Crystal said sadly, "that he'd

be like all the others. Shunning someone with such a history. Oh, I knew he was smart enough not to be convinced of the bad gene theory, or at least I hoped he was, but when he asked me to marry him, I didn't dare take the chance. Do you see? I'd never expected anyone like Jeff to come along, to see me as normal, human, hungry for all the things other women had. I *knew* I should tell him, but I couldn't."

What would I have done under those circumstances? Become a mental case myself, probably, I thought honestly.

"And now I've ruined everything," she said. "If I couldn't tell him when I should have, he'll never forgive me now."

To my horror, she started to cry in earnest, bending forward, sobbing into her hands.

"Of course he'll forgive you!" I blurted. "*You* didn't murder anybody! Crystal"—was this the first time I'd called her by her name?—"Dad's a Christian! He believes in what Jesus taught, that we forgive even our enemies, seventy times seven! How can you believe he won't understand when he learns everything that's happened?"

She lifted her dripping face. "But you're having a hard time forgiving me for marrying your father," she said.

I felt as if I'd been body-slammed. Shame surged

through me, and Buster pushed harder against me, turning to nuzzle under my armpit.

I couldn't think of any words in my own defense. She was telling the truth. *I* hadn't even forgiven once, let alone seventy times seven.

"How am I going to tell him what he had a right to know before he ever married me?"

I struggled for words. "The same way you told me, I guess." And then, seeing her desolate expression, I suggested, "Do you want me to tell him? Most of the basics, anyway, and then you can fill in the details—any you want to share—later?"

Hope flickered in her blue eyes. "Would you? Would you, Nikki?"

I hugged Buster hard and said, "Sure." I hesitated before asking the question that had been forming in my mind. "Your uncle, the one who . . . hurt everybody. Cecil B. Gyasi. Do you know if the *B* stands for *Bruce?*"

Consternation swept over her as she knotted her hands into fists on her thighs. "Oh, my God. Is he *there? Now? In the house where you've been working?*"

My silence was eloquent, which was a good thing because I was back to being unable to speak.

"I thought they'd locked him up forever! Where he could never hurt anyone again! You've *seen* him?"

"They call him Bruce now, and they say he's the gardener."

Bewildered, frightened, she pounded with her fists. "How could they let him go free? How could he be right over there, almost next door to us? Oh, dear God, I knew I never should have come back here! I had no idea he was free, and I didn't want to come back, but I couldn't make Jeff understand, not without telling him—why on earth did Aunt Edna leave her house to *me?*"

"Because you were the only one left?" I suggested softly, and finally I was able to reach for her, to hug her the way Dad would have done if he were here.

After awhile I asked, "What am I going to do? I don't think I can go back there to finish the typing job."

"No," Crystal agreed. "No. We'd better try to call your father."

"I tried, earlier. I didn't get an answer. I left a message, though. Maybe he'll call us when he gets home, even if it's late."

When we finally went downstairs, I don't know how much later, an enticing aroma drifted up to meet us. The boys were still playing their game, but the table was set in the dining room.

"What's cooking?" I asked in amazement.

"You left that recipe and all the stuff to fix it on the counter," Sam said, "so we decided to make chicken pot pie." He shot a glance at Crystal. "I'm sorry about your hair."

"So am I," Crystal said wearily. "Nikki thinks your dad will forgive me."

"Prob'ly," Sam decided after a moment. "He forgave me for borrowing his favorite CD and losing it. And he only bawled me out a little bit when I broke my arm skateboarding after he told me not to do it. That was *after* the cast was on it."

Neither Crystal nor I was very hungry, at least at first, but the boys were starving and there wasn't much left of the casserole. My mind kept racing. How could I possibly finish the typing job? How could I even return to the house and tell Mr. Gyasi why?

I tried the phone again after we'd eaten. I got the answering machine at the house.

"Daddy," I said, "we need you. Call us immediately." I couldn't very well add a reassuring message that everything was all right. "Even if it's really late, call us, and let the phone ring until we can get downstairs to answer it."

The evening passed with no phone call. This evening, Crystal didn't retreat to her room and close the door. She built a fire in the living-room fireplace, and watched the boys as they sprawled on the floor with yet another board game. I tried to read and couldn't. *Please, Dad, call!* I kept thinking.

Around eight o'clock, the wind came up and the rain began to beat against the windows. Around nine, when we were sending Jeremy and Sam up to bed, there was a tremendous booming crash that brought us all to attention, including poor, deaf Buster.

"Thunder," Crystal said when our ears stopped ringing.

It rains a lot in the Pacific northwest, but we don't often have thunder and lightning with it, so it took a bit of getting used to as it continued to rumble overhead. When the lights flickered, then steadied, Crystal stood up. "I think we'd better prepare for a power outage. Jeff brought flashlights. They're in a drawer in the kitchen. Would you get them, Nikki? I'll make sure the kerosene lamps are ready to go."

Twenty minutes after we'd returned to the living room, the house went black and stayed that way.

We gave the boys one flashlight and lighted two lamps. When I tested the phone, the line was dead.

Crystal and I looked at one another. What would Dad think when he tried to call and the line was down?

There was nothing to do. Neither of us wanted to go to bed, yet reading was impossible. There was no hope of a phone call from Dad. There was no solution to the problem of what to do about my job in the morning.

With the electricity off, the furnace wasn't running.

Crystal put a couple more chunks of wood on the fire, because it was chilly, even in July. Though neither of us had ever started a fire in a wood range, we thought we'd better do that, too. Luckily there was a woodbox in the kitchen, with kindling and old newspapers.

"Maybe we should each take a couch and just stay down here for the night, or at least until the power comes back on," she suggested at last.

It seemed better than ascending the stairs into a pitch-black second floor and separating. We left one lamp burning, low, and had another one ready to light if and when we needed it. Buster curled up in front of the fireplace and began to snore.

I don't know what time it was when I was awakened with a resounding crash directly overhead, strong enough to make the house vibrate around us. Crystal, too, sat up. "That sounded close," she said. "I hope it didn't scare the boys."

"I suppose part of taking care of them is making sure," I said. "Maybe we'd better go check on them."

Neither of us commented on the fact that we had somehow become a team, unwilling to go wandering around on our own. We went up the stairs and found the boys dead to the world. That was a common expression, but in the light of what Crystal had told me tonight, it seemed a gruesome thought.

"I think I'll get a sweatshirt," I said, and stepped into my own room. The night beyond the windows was intensely black, and then there was yet another thunderboomer, this time accompanied by a visible flash of lightning.

I stood for a moment, shrugging into the sweatshirt, while Crystal waited for me in the doorway. I frowned, pressing my face against the cold glass, seeing nothing out over the ocean. I thought about the ships out there—the little boats would have made for shore hours ago—and wondered how safe they were.

And then something on the edge of my vision caught my attention. "Crystal—" I said uncertainly.

"Yes?" She came into the room, hugging herself against the chill that was quite noticeable up here without the furnace.

"Over there—toward the Gyasi house. I thought I saw a flicker of light. Not electric light, it wasn't steady enough for that—"

She, too, pressed her face against the glass. "They've probably lighted lamps too, and someone's carrying one around."

"That last flash of lightning was really close. Could it have hit their tower?"

"Fire?" she said, frowning.

"Let's look from our own tower," I said, and swiveled the flashlight to lead the way.

From our third-floor level, there was no question about it. There was an unsteady glow in the tower windows at the Gyasi house. More than a lamp or a lantern.

"We can't call them. Or the fire department," I breathed, reaching for the glasses. "It's fire, Crystal. That's Bruce's room, up there at the top. I was up there when Julian showed me around this morning."

She hesitated only a moment. "I'd better get the car out and run for town to notify the fire department."

We clattered down the stairs, making enough noise that we finally aroused the boys.

"What's going on?" Sam called out.

"We think lightning may have hit the tower at the Gyasi house," I told him. "We're going to run into Trinidad to notify the fire department. You guys want to come in your pajamas, or stay in bed?"

"Stay in bed," they both voted. "Leave Buster!"

We ran on down the stairs. We hadn't brought any rain gear of our own, but Aunt Edna had assorted slickers, two of them with hoods. We grabbed them and dashed outside into an icy, driving rain that sluiced over everything not covered with waterproofing; our feet were instantly soaked.

We reached the car and piled in, and Crystal turned on the ignition and the lights, and put it into reverse to turn around.

Twenty yards down the drive, she slammed on the brakes.

A gigantic tree completely blocked the way.

Both of us cried out in dismay. "There's no way around it," Crystal wailed. "We're trapped!"

15

"We'll have to go by the beach," I said, opening the car door.

Her face was pasty under the dome light. "Nikki, we can't."

"We have to," I said, though I was shaking with fear as much as cold. "Mrs. Mallory goes home at night, but Julian's on the second floor, and Mr. Gyasi's in a wheelchair on the ground floor. And Bruce sleeps in the tower. If they don't wake up, they'll all die."

She cut the engine and piled out of the car. "We'll never make it in time."

I had the flashlight on, already running toward the stairs. "Maybe we can. Mrs. Mallory said the house is made of redwood, and it's fire-resistant, so maybe that will slow it down. The fire was so far only in the tower, and fire burns up, doesn't it? It may be too late for Bruce, but we might still save the others."

She ran with me, making little protesting noises, but keeping up. Before we started down, she said, "I can't, Nikki. I can't."

"Then I'll have to go alone," I said, knowing I'd never live with myself if I didn't try.

She couldn't have been any more terrified than I was, but by the time I'd gone down a dozen steps I knew she was behind me. I wished we had Buster, but there wasn't time to get him.

I nearly fell several times, with the flashlight bobbing its glow ahead of us. The wind was almost enough to knock us down, and the surf had never sounded so loud or so fierce. At the bottom of the stairs, I reached around for Crystal's hand, and we turned sort of crossways of the wind.

"The tide has probably covered the rock," Crystal said, gasping. "We won't be able to get around it."

I didn't waste breath answering. If the high tide prevented us from reaching the other house, we would have done all we could.

The rock loomed ahead of us in the bobbing light. I

had a stitch in my side now, and Crystal was holding herself, too, but we kept moving. The water foamed up over the sand, dashing against the rock, but it looked to me as if we could still wade through it.

"We'll never get back this way. The tide will cut us off," Crystal said, yet she followed me into the curling water, up to our ankles, our knees—how much deeper could we go?

We were wet to our hips in frigid water by the time we rounded the rocky obstruction. And there, above us, dominating the night, was the tall Victorian with flames coming through the roof of the tower now. So far, there was no sign of fire below it.

Please, God, let us get them out, I prayed as we ran toward the second flight of stairs.

I don't know what kept us going to the top. We were exhausted, staggering across the yard, and I stumbled into the side of the van and shone the light inside to determine that the keys were in the ignition. Thank God for country people who weren't paranoid about having their cars stolen if they left the keys in them. At least we'd have a way out of here without having to brave the high tide. If there weren't any trees down across *this* driveway.

Crystal jerked open the door and slid inside, turning

on headlights that cut through the downpour with minimal effect. By the time I reached the house, however, my stepmother was right behind me.

I twisted the bell and heard the sound inside, over and over. Hoping against hope, I tried the knob, and the door opened under my hand. "Thank God for country people who don't lock their houses, either," I muttered, and stepped into the hallway.

I tried the wall switch but found, as I expected, that the power was off here, too. I yelled as loudly as I could. "Fire! Your house is on fire! Get up! Get out!"

There was no response.

"Oh, please, God," Crystal panted beside me, "don't let him have done it again!"

That hadn't even occurred to me. I couldn't allow myself to dwell on it. "We'll have to stick together with only one light," I said. "Mr. Gyasi's bedroom is back along the main hall."

"There are probably more flashlights somewhere in a drawer in the kitchen," Crystal said, which was pretty good thinking for someone in her advanced state of terror. "I don't remember where it is."

"Off to the right. Feel your way through the dining room, then it opens into the kitchen. The cabinets with drawers are mostly on the left." I prayed silently that there wasn't a madman in this house as well as the fire on the top floor, and ran, my shoes squishing, to pound on Mr. Gyasi's bedroom door. "Wake up!" I shouted. "The house is on fire!"

After a few seconds, I heard him. "Who's there? Who is it?"

"It's Nikki! The lightning struck your tower, and it's burning! The phones are out and we couldn't call for the fire department! You need to get out! I'll go wake up Julian!"

"Yes. Yes, go," he said, sounding fully awake now. "And Bruce is up there, too, in the tower."

Unless Bruce had already escaped, it was too late for him, I thought. I didn't stand around to argue, but ran back the way I'd come.

I met Crystal at the foot of the stairs, a flashlight in her hand. "What shall I do?" she asked, as if I were the grown-up and she the child. What was going through her mind now? Did she remember anything about this house except the horror of the night her parents had died here?

"I'm going upstairs. Julian's room faces the ocean. I'll yell up the tower stairs. Maybe you can help Mr. Gyasi get outside."

She hurried unhesitatingly back the way I'd come,

and I raced up the stairs. It was still pitch-black, no sign of fire on this floor, but I could smell the smoke now. "Julian!" I screamed. "The house is on fire!"

He came awake quickly, appearing in his doorway with his own flashlight. He'd pulled on a pair of jeans and was struggling into a sweatshirt, not bothering with shoes. As he came into the upper hallway, there was an explosive sound, and the flames appeared above us, the smell now in a matter of seconds overpowering.

"We've got to get out fast," I said, and wondered if I'd later feel guilty that I hadn't attempted to reach Bruce, if he was still up there. Yet I knew it was useless, too late. It was an inferno above this level.

"We have to get Dad," Julian said as we nearly fell down the stairway in our haste.

"Crystal's with him," I said, almost out of breath.

We saw their bobbing lights toward the front of the house. Crystal cried, "He insists he's got to save his manuscript! Go on, get out of the house! We're coming!"

The fire roared now, a thing alive, penetrating the gloom of the stairway and lower hall. Julian ran past me, yelling for his father, and a moment later the four of us were skidding down the ramp.

It was still raining buckets, and I was freezing, but all that mattered was getting away from the house. We were halfway across the yard when the flames shot out through the roof—the second floor, not the tower, which was already a total loss. Debris rained down onto the veranda overhang and the yard as we piled into the car. Crystal had it turning, accelerating, before anyone thought to reach for a seat belt.

"I saved my manuscript, but I couldn't do anything about the computer," Hudson Gyasi said. "I'm afraid the house is gone, boy. We're homeless again."

"We're alive," Julian pointed out. "What about Bruce? There was no way to get to him if he was still in the tower."

Nobody answered.

Half a mile toward town, we met the fire trucks. Crystal was able to pull off into a side road to let the trucks go past. "Somebody must have seen the fire from town," she said, moving ahead again. "There's a tree down across our driveway; I can't get us there until someone cuts it out of the way."

"There are motels at Trinidad," Mr. Gyasi said. "We'd better go there. I grabbed my wallet with my credit cards. Did you get anything out, Julian?"

"My pants and a sweatshirt," Julian said. "Not even my guitar."

As we pulled out onto the highway, we nearly collided head-on with another car. In the headlights we recognized the other driver through our rain-slashed windows as he pulled alongside us. "Dad!" I screamed over the howl of the wind, and he bailed out and ran toward us.

Crystal dove out into the storm too, and ran into his arms, where they were getting soaked even further. Somehow, I didn't begrudge her that hug. I got the second one.

"I met the fire trucks coming from town, and I was afraid it was our place. And then they went past our road and when I tried to go in that driveway, I couldn't get past that fallen tree except on foot. I saw you'd abandoned our van with the lights still on, and when I got in the house, the boys told me the Gyasi place was on fire, so I figured that was where you'd gone. Is everybody okay?"

"We're trying to take them to a motel," Crystal said, her teeth chattering. "Can you follow us there?"

Hudson Gyasi directed us to the motel, where the power was off, but Julian ran ahead to open the door, and there were people there, voices and flashlights, coming to help.

Thank you, God, I breathed, and I meant for Dad coming, and the Gyasis' escape, and the fact that Crystal and I hadn't been trapped by that wicked incoming tide.

By this time, the ramp came out of the van and Mr. Gyasi rolled down it, clutching his manuscript box, which he had hastily covered with a plastic bag.

Dad had pulled in behind us and come running over to the open window beside Crystal. He was bareheaded, and water streamed over him as if he were under a waterfall.

"Thank God you're here," Crystal said, clutching the arm he leaned into the opening.

"You said you needed me, and there was no plane scheduled to fly in here from Seattle yet tonight," Dad said. "Your phone was out, and I imagined every kind of horrible emergency. When I checked with the sheriff's department, they said the county was being hard hit by a storm. So I chartered a plane and flew as far as I could. They let us land at Crescent City, and I rented a car after that. I'll figure out how to pay for all this when I make sure everybody's okay. Does anyone need a doctor? A hospital?"

"No." My teeth were chattering so I could hardly talk. "We just need to go home and get warm and dry."

The rental car was still standing, lights on, motor running. "Okay. Change cars, we'll leave their van here. I'll go check on the Gyasis, make sure they don't need anything else, and we'll go home. We can walk in from the roadblock until we can get somebody out tomorrow with chain saws."

I got in the rear seat, and Crystal sat up front with Dad. He didn't notice her hair until we'd tramped through the storm, still seeing flames from farther up the beach over the tops of the black trees, and entered the house. The boys, dressed in jeans and sweatshirts, were in the kitchen, with a lighted kerosene lamp. Eating, of all things.

"Hey, what took you so long?" Sam demanded. "We put some more wood in the stove."

I think Crystal had forgotten her hair. She pushed back the rubberized hood and was shrugging out of the borrowed coat when Dad got a good look at her.

"Well," he said into the sudden silence, "I'm going to be interested in the explanation for *that*."

"See?" Sam said cheerfully. "I knew he wouldn't *really* kill you."

"We need to get out of these wet shoes and jeans," I said, "before anybody explains anything."

There were clean jeans and socks on top of the dryer for Crystal and me; we stripped and changed right there, while Dad settled for a dry flannel shirt and a pair of walking shorts that were the only things available without going upstairs. He piled more wood on the open fire in the living room, then sprawled back on the couch, pulling Crystal down with him and holding on to her hand.

"Did you get everybody out of that burning house?" he asked.

"Not Bruce—the gardener, or whoever he was. Mr. Gyasi's brother, I guess. We didn't see any sign of him. It was his room, at the top of the tower."

"I'm sorry about that. You tried, I guess. You must have run all the way over there by the beach." Dad looked at Crystal. "I think I'm braced to find out why my beautiful blond bride now looks as if somebody dumped mud over her head."

Crystal cast me an imploring glance, and I swallowed. "Well, it's a very long story. And I told her I'd help explain it to you. Sam, make us some hot cocoa. This is going to take awhile, and we're all half-frozen."

"I want to hear," Sam protested. But Dad reminded us, "How's he going to make hot cocoa if the power's off? It'd take a long time to heat it on that wood range. What is so difficult that Crystal can't tell me about it herself?"

"I tried," Crystal said with an effort. "I tried to tell you I didn't want to come here, I never should have. I should have *insisted*—"

He squeezed her hand. "You ruined your hair because we came here? Sweetie, when does this start to make sense?"

I gathered my courage. "After you hear the whole story. Without interrupting. Dad, you are going to have to learn to listen to her. You don't *listen.*"

He appeared affronted. "I don't?"

"No. She had a terrible reason for not wanting to come here, and you talked right on top of her, and went ahead and packed, and we came. You never *listened.*"

"Okay. I'm listening now," he said, and he did.

Not totally without interruptions. Not without putting an arm around Crystal and hugging her up against his side. And when he heard about Bruce, he nearly lost it for a moment.

"You mean he talked us into letting my daughter go to work there, knowing his brother, who had slaughtered a whole family twenty years ago, was there in the house, without telling us?"

I wasn't too comfortable with that myself. "I guess Bruce didn't have anywhere else to go. When he got out of prison, or the mental hospital, or ran away from it, or whatever he did."

Crystal spoke for the first time at this point. "I don't suppose he could have gone to work anywhere else, with the record he had. But they had no right to let Nikki go to work there, under the circumstances."

Dad was scowling. "But both the minister and the deputy verified his legitimacy. Surely they were aware of the story of that family and that house, even twenty years after everything happened there."

"I don't think anybody knew that Bruce was the brother who did it, who'd been locked up in a mental hospital all that time," I offered. "They kept him more or less out of sight, and they called him by his middle name. I don't think even Julian or Mrs. Mallory knew he was a relative."

"I'm afraid Mr. Gyasi and I are going to have a serious talk about the ethics of hiring my fourteen-year-old daughter to work in that house under those circumstances. Do you think this Bruce set the fire tonight?" Dad asked.

"We're pretty sure it was a lightning strike," I said. "We didn't see it hit, but we spotted the fire right after a terrific flash."

He opened his mouth to ask something else, and I got out of my chair and walked over to him, putting my face no more than six inches from his.

"Dad. When Mom wanted you to shut up, she told you so. Crystal isn't going to be like that. She has to learn a new technique." I reached out and took hold of both his ears, holding his head still so we were eyeball to eyeball. "Like this, Crystal. Hold his ears and speak distinctly while he can't see anything but your face. And say, *Be quiet, Jeff, and listen to me.*"

"Okay," Dad said when I let go of his ears. "I get the message. Give me the rest of the story."

It took a bit longer. And we let him ask the questions afterward, and Crystal still wasn't helping much with the answers, but he was still holding her hand and had an arm around her.

"I blew it six ways from Sunday, didn't I?" he said finally. "I'm sorry, sweetie. I didn't realize I was walking all over you. Maybe Nikki's method would work, though maybe we'd better try for a way you can clue me in in public without making us look like idiots."

He stood up, pulling Crystal with him. "I never got any dinner tonight. Is there anything to eat around here that doesn't have to be heated up?"

We didn't finish talking and get to sleep until almost 3 A.M. Crystal was still shivering. Somehow Buster had helped to warm her a little bit by leaning against her side, but when we got up from the table where we'd watched Dad eat cold canned peaches and a salami sandwich, she said, "I don't think I'll ever be warm again."

We slept late, waking to full sunshine and a Pacific that lived up to its name: brilliant blue, and with only a gentle, rolling surf. It seemed impossible that only a few hours ago a wild storm had raged.

The power was still off. No doubt the fallen tree continued to block the driveway.

I dressed quickly, needing the warmth of my socks and sweatshirt with jeans, and after a brief stop in the bathroom, I ran up the stairs into the tower.

I didn't need the binoculars to see that the taller tower on the Gyasi house was gone. What I could see of the roof below it showed gaping holes. But I was astonished to see that the house itself had not been totally destroyed. Would there be enough left to rebuild, or would that beautiful old house, the scene of so much horror, have to be completely torn down?

I'd never lived through a fire. Never lost a home. Yet I knew instinctively that the loss would be as devastating as the loss of a parent, the loss of so many things one held very dear. I wondered if anything on the second floor of the house had survived, if Julian's guitar and his books might still be salvaged. The Gyasis had come here because they'd had nowhere else to go, no money to pay for housing elsewhere, and this house had belonged to them and so offered a refuge. They had finished out the night in a motel, but where would they go now?

Somewhere nearby, I heard a chain saw start up. I put down the glasses on the window ledge and ran down the stairs and into the kitchen.

Pancakes. I smelled pancakes. The kitchen was a disaster area, with bowls and spoons and cups all over the counter, and spilled batter everywhere, including the floor, but Sam and Jeremy were at the table, each with a stack of hotcakes on their plates. "We found a package of pancake flour," Sam said proudly. "It's easy. All you have to do is add water."

"Great. Did Dad get through to someone to come cut up the tree across the driveway?"

"No. He found a chain saw that belonged to Aunt Edna, so he's out there working on it. As soon as we get through eating, we have to go help haul the cut-up logs away so we can get the car through."

Remembering, I looked at the stove. "Is the electricity back on now?"

"Ten minutes ago," my little brother confirmed.

"And you did all this damage in ten minutes?" I asked, incredulous. "You are going to clean it up before you go outside, aren't you?"

"Dad needs our help. Besides, when Crystal wakes up, she'll probably want some pancakes, too. And Dad, when he's finished with the chain saw. No sense cleaning up before everybody's had something to eat," Sam pointed out logically.

So, naturally, I got to be the one who cleaned up. Crystal came down half an hour after I did, and except for the mud-colored hair, she looked a lot better than last night. She didn't say anything, but I could tell by her manner that she and Dad had worked things out.

"I'm going to start packing things up to go home," she said. "Jeff's going to talk to a realtor about putting this place on the market. He wants to check on the Gyasis, too, before we go. But we'll be out of here by mid-afternoon at the latest."

I was eager to go, yet at the same time I felt a twinge of regret for the lost beach. I never got to spend much time on it except racing back and forth when I was scared spitless.

Crystal looked at me over her glass of carrot juice, smiling ever so faintly. "When this place sells, and Jeff thinks it should easily do so, we'll have enough money to buy another vacation place. On a beach, if you like, but closer to home, so we can go there more often."

"Good," I said.

And so Dad cut up enough of the tree so we could drive out, and he brought papers for Crystal to sign to sell the place—she still didn't want to go out in public—and he stopped at the motel and talked to Hudson Gyasi.

"I had trouble concealing my hostility at not being told about Bruce, and what he'd done in that house," Dad reported. "I understand that when the man was released, and had nowhere to go and no way to support himself, his brother felt he had to take him in. But it was irresponsible to allow Nikki to go there to work, without clueing us in on the true situation. I doubt if young Julian or the housekeeper knew about his criminal past."

"I don't suppose I'll ever get paid for the work I did, will I?" I said.

"Afraid not. Maybe when we get home you can find a part-time job in the neighborhood."

"Yeah," I agreed. "Delivering advertising flyers, or baby-sitting the Lindquist kids." There were six of them, and they were notorious for their escapades, several of which had resulted in calling an aid car, a fire truck with a tall ladder, or the police. I'd never sat them, but Bonnie had.

I never got to say good-bye to Julian. We learned later that the front part of the second floor had not been completely destroyed, though he'd lost both the guitar and a lot of his books. Anyway, he went away to school in the fall. I wondered if he, like Crystal, would be followed by the family history, and if he'd be strong enough to surmount it.

They did rebuild, with the insurance money. The realtor eventually reported that to Dad when Aunt Edna's house was sold to a big family eager to live on a cliff overlooking a virtually private beach.

They didn't find Bruce's body in the burned-out part of the building. There was nothing left of the tower, so it was impossible to know if he'd taken his clothes or anything when he'd escaped.

I never got to the point where I could think of Crystal as my mom. And *stepmother* seemed too negative a thing, too, so when I introduce her, I call her "Crystal, my dad's new wife."

It's okay with her if we have kids over to the house and serve whatever we want as refreshments. We always turn down her offers of carrot juice, though the fruit and whole-grain crackers are good.

I thought about Julian for a long time. Until October, when I met Joe Madison, a tenth grader who played baseball, and helped me with my math while I tutored him in English. I had a good time that year with Joe and learned to appreciate the finer points of sporting events.

I know Julian and I had connected, for just a few minutes, when we were looking at his favorite books and knew they were my favorites, too.

Someday, I thought, I'll meet someone else like Julian. A guy who likes the same books I do, a guy I can really talk to, about anything. The way Crystal now talks to

Dad. I hear them sometimes, late at night, whispering and giggling. Yes, giggling, even Crystal.

A wonderful man, Crystal had called him. Strong, and funny, and affectionate. Responsible. Responsible is important.

I don't know if Joe Madison is all those things, or if I'll have to keep looking.

But I'm sure of one thing.

He's out there, somewhere, and he's looking for me.

I said that to Crystal the other day, and she smiled and ran a hand through her grown-back-to-normal silvery hair.

"He'll find you, Nikki," she promised, and for a moment we stood there, smiling at each other.